"Kayla? Are you okay?"

Jude quickly moved to her side. Had her passing out done something to the baby?

She faced him, her chestnut eyes suddenly alight. "I think I just felt the baby move." She placed her other hand beside the first, her smile growing wide. "There it is again."

Kayla reached for Jude's hand and pressed it against her protruding belly. "Do you feel it?"

He hesitated at first, wanting to pull away, but not wanting to hurt her feelings. Then he felt it. The slightest kick beneath his fingers.

His own eyes widened. "You might have a punter in there."

She set her hand next to his. "Or a soccer player."

Looking into Kayla's eyes, Jude wasn't sure he'd ever experienced a more precious moment in his life. And as he watched her, one thing became perfectly clear.

He would do everything in his power to protect Kayla and her baby.

It took **Mindy Obenhaus** forty years to figure out what she wanted to do when she grew up. But once God called her to write, she never looked back. She's passionate about touching readers with biblical truths in an entertaining, and sometimes adventurous, manner. Mindy lives in Texas with her husband and kids. When she's not writing, she enjoys cooking and spending time with her grandchildren. Find more at mindyobenhaus.com.

Books by Mindy Obenhaus

Love Inspired

Rocky Mountain Heroes

Their Ranch Reunion
The Deputy's Holiday Family
Her Colorado Cowboy
Reunited in the Rockies

The Doctor's Family Reunion
Rescuing the Texan's Heart
A Father's Second Chance
Falling for the Hometown Hero

Visit the Author Profile page at Harlequin.com.

Reunited in the Rockies

Mindy Obenhaus

HARLEQUIN® LOVE INSPIRED®

Recycling programs
for this product may
not exist in your area.

LOVE INSPIRED BOOKS

ISBN-13: 978-1-335-42902-5

Reunited in the Rockies

Copyright © 2019 by Melinda Obenhaus

www.Harlequin.com

Printed in U.S.A.

Beareth all things, believeth all things, hopeth all things, endureth all things.

—*1 Corinthians* 13:7

For Your glory, Lord.

Acknowledgments

To Cheryl Leyendecker, thank you
for your friendship and enduring
countless questions about cattle ranching.

To Betty Wolfe, thanks for putting up with me.

To Richard, the best support system
a girl could ask for.

Chapter One

Twenty-four hours ago, Jude Stephens had his life figured out.

Then his father started talking about retirement, and he clearly viewed Jude as the heir apparent to the business he'd spent decades building.

Hands clutched around the steering wheel of his police SUV, Jude made another pass down Ouray, Colorado's Main Street, looking for anything out of place among the rows of quaint Victorian-era buildings. He was honored that his father thought so highly of him that he was willing to entrust him with the business he'd started with nothing more than a dream and a small patch of land. Problem was, Jude did not want to be a cattle rancher.

Clouds obscured the sun, spoiling what should have been a beautiful October day. Helping his father out was one thing; he'd done it all his life. But the man had four other sons. Why not turn the business over to one of them?

Jude drummed his fingers on the dash. Because he was the one Dad counted on while his brothers were out chasing their dreams.

He shook his head. Just because he was the only brother who had never left Ouray didn't mean he didn't have dreams, too. If only his father would recognize his wood-working for the viable business it was instead of just a hobby. Jude was passionate about the work he was doing, and his custom and reproduction millwork was already providing him with more income than his job as a police officer. He'd even talked with the chief about his desire to resign. He was simply waiting until they hired another officer. Then he'd be free to focus on *his* business and take it to the next level.

But first he'd have to find a way to tell Clint Stephens he wanted no part of his cattle operation. And with the man getting older, that wasn't going to be easy. That bout of pneumonia he'd had last year had everyone concerned.

Passing the hot springs pool, he roughed a hand over his face. Couldn't his father just sell off the cows and leave Jude to follow his own path? Dad knew all about dreams, after all. He'd chased his own all those years ago when he and Mama first started Abundant Blessings Ranch. Now, Jude's oldest brother, Noah, had built a successful rodeo school on the land, and Jude longed to do the same with his business. All he needed was a bigger shop. Something he was more than capable of paying for.

So when are you planning to tell the man?

Good question. He should have said something about his plans to resign after talking to the chief. But he hadn't. Now he was faced with the very real threat of disappointing his dad. And just the thought of that nearly killed him. The last thing he wanted was to destroy the good relationship they had.

He straightened in his seat. Lately he'd been doing a fair amount of work for a builder in Telluride. Maybe that would help his father understand. Unfortunately, the majority of his sales were done online, and that was something his father couldn't comprehend, no matter how many times a week that big brown shipping truck came rolling up the drive.

He wound past the sparsely populated RV park that had been bursting at the seams only a couple of months ago. Perhaps Noah would have some advice. Despite their eleven-year age difference, he and his eldest brother were quite close. Close enough that Noah had asked him to be his best man.

Jamming his fingers through his hair, Jude released a frustrated sigh. He was going to drive himself crazy if he kept dwelling on his father. He needed to think about something else. Like the meeting with his soon-to-be sister-in-law, Lily. He didn't have a clue as to why she'd asked him to meet her at the old Congress Hotel after work. The historic building had been closed for years and fallen into disrepair. Was Lily thinking about buying it? Restoring it, perhaps? If anyone could afford to do that, it was her. And in the right hands, the once grand structure definitely had the potential to be magnificent yet again.

He eased into Rotary Park to make his usual turnaround, noting a blue pickup truck near the ice rink. Not out of the ordinary. However, the woman standing beside the vehicle, staring at a flat tire, was a call to action.

Her back was to him as he pulled up beside her. Silky dark brown hair fell to her waist, reminding him of someone he once knew. Someone he'd never forget.

Killing the engine, he continued to watch her. Even her stance was familiar. The way she stood with her hands perched on the backside of her hips.

His heart raced. What if it was her?

You wish.

He reached for the door handle. His mind was all kinds of messed up today. As if Kayla would suddenly show up in Ouray after seven years.

The woman glanced over her shoulder as he stepped onto the gravel, though not long enough to give him a good look.

"I see you're having a problem." He rounded the front end of his vehicle, glimpsing her pancaked back tire. "May I assist you?"

Slowly she turned, and his world shifted as though he'd been transported back in time to the best summer of his life. The summer he fell in love for the first and only time.

"Hello, Jude." The sweetness of her voice washed over him, along with more memories and regrets than he cared to count.

"Kayla?" He visually traced the face that still lived in his mind. All these years, he'd wondered what had happened. He only knew that one day they were talking about seeing each other again, and then the next there was nothing. She had never even returned his calls or texts. "What are you doing here?"

She hesitated a moment, seemingly transfixed on the tire. "My friend is getting married." Her chestnut eyes finally met his. Gorgeous eyes he'd lost himself in thousands of times. "I'm Lily's matron of honor."

"Lily?" Wait, Noah's Lily? Shifting his weight from one booted foot to the other, he scratched his head. "Lily Davis?"

A breeze hissed through the towering conifers.

"Yes." Kayla casually tucked her hair behind her ear, the reappearing sun highlighting the gold band on her left hand.

His gut tightened as unwanted disappointment stole through him. After all these years, he shouldn't care that Kayla was married. Not when she was the one who'd decided to end their relationship without even bothering to let him know. No, he shouldn't care.

Unfortunately, he did. A fact that annoyed him more than he cared to admit.

Her hand fell to her stomach. Only then did he notice the bump beneath her fitted T-shirt.

Great. The woman who still haunted his dreams was not only married but pregnant. And she was his future sister-in-law's best friend. The one he'd be forced to spend who knows how much time with in the coming days before walking her down the aisle a week from tomorrow.

He should have stayed in bed this morning. "You and Lily are friends?"

"Yes. We met back in Denver a few years ago."

"You live in Denver?" When he'd known her, she'd been enjoying a nomadic lifestyle with her parents. Always roaming about the country, never staying put for more than six months. They were headed to Denver the last time he and Kayla spoke. Had she been there all this time?

"After my father died, I decided it was time to settle down."

She couldn't have done that in Ouray? "I'm sorry for your loss."

Nodding, she took a step back. "Look, I'm sorry for creating such an awkward situation. I knew Noah was your brother, yet I never said anything to Lily about you and me. If I had, she could have at least prepared you."

True. And he could have relegated his best man duties to one of his brothers while he hightailed it out of town. "No big deal." He shrugged. "I'm just kind of surprised you're here so early. I mean, the wedding isn't for another week."

"I wanted to be here to help Lily with some of the preparations." Her hands went to her hips again as her gaze traveled from the redstone cliffs that hugged the back of the park to Mount Hayden's peak at the opposite end of town. "That and I needed a change of scenery."

"Well, we've got plenty of that around here." Though he had no business doing it, he found himself staring again. She was even more beautiful than he remembered. Yet while the hair and eyes were the same, something was different about Kayla. She seemed…troubled. Maybe it was just the awkwardness of the moment.

Shaking off the notion, he added, "But then, you already know that."

She peered up at him through long lashes, sending his heart slamming into his ribs. "I wasn't sure if you were still in Ouray."

Wasn't sure? Kayla knew better than anyone that this was where he belonged. "It's my home. Where my roots are." And while that was the exact reason he could never leave, it was also what had prevented him from asking her to stay. Kayla needed to roam, meaning their relationship would have been doomed from the start and he would have ended up brokenhearted anyway.

Looking for an escape, he turned his attention to her tire. "I'll get this taken care of so you can be on your way."

"You always were the chivalrous one." Her smile did strange things to him. Had him feeling things he had no business feeling for a married woman. Things that were going to make this next week excruciatingly long.

Kayla Bradshaw had known that agreeing to be in Lily's wedding could mean coming face-to-face with the first man she ever loved. Something that seemed relatively benign, until now.

Jude still had that slightly dangerous look about him. Those piercing dark eyes that seemed to see right through her. To read her thoughts and know her heart. His dark hair had a military cut with close-cropped sides and the longer top brushed to one side. But, oh, that smile...

Pulling out of the park with a fresh tire, she gave herself a stern shake. It wasn't like her to be so affected. Then again, a lot of things were different with her lately. Chalk it up to pregnancy. Or stress. After all, when her husband died five months ago in a single-car rollover, she hadn't even known she was pregnant.

She continued into the old mining town, eyeing the mountains that enveloped Ouray. She hoped God forgave her for the relief she felt following Shane's death.

If only she'd known he was an alcoholic before they married. He was a different man when he drank.

After his death, she'd wanted nothing more than a do-over. A fresh start for her and her baby. And while she had yet to find that perfect place to begin anew, Lily had done her best to fill in the gap.

When Kayla decided to sell the house she'd shared with Shane, Lily had encouraged her to move into her place and house-sit while she and her kids spent the summer in Ouray. Four months later, she was still there.

Kayla puffed out a laugh. She never would have imagined that her friend would decide to stay in Ouray, let alone fall in love with the brother of the man who'd captured Kayla's heart seven years ago and given her a glimpse of how good life could really be.

She was surprised, if not a little disappointed, to see that Jude was a police officer, though. With his woodworking talents and love for historic buildings, she'd thought for sure he'd follow his passion.

Slowing her speed as she entered town, she tried to ignore the question that had been plaguing her brain. But like a nasty mosquito bite, it refused to be ignored. Was Jude married?

Not that it mattered. Their time together was water under the bridge. He'd made that clear during their last phone conversation. He'd said he was done. Then he'd hung up. And she never had the opportunity to talk to him again.

She had no doubt Jude assumed she was married, though. The way his gaze moved from her left hand to her baby bump.

Taking in Ouray's Main Street, she was happy to see not all that much had changed. Sure, the names on some of the businesses were different, the paint colors may have been altered, but the essence of the town remained the same. Warm, inviting... The kind of place she'd longed for her entire life. A place she could not only call home, but where she felt at home.

Looking back, she wished she'd had the guts to tell her parents to leave Ouray without her. But she'd been too immature.

In Denver, though, she'd finally put her foot down, thinking that staying there would satisfy her desire. No more traveling around the country in an RV. Then she'd married and Shane owned a house. Something she'd never had. Yet her longing was far from fulfilled, and her dream turned into a nightmare.

If only she'd made better choices. If only—

"Would you stop thinking about Jude already?" Pounding her fist against the steering wheel, she made a left turn onto one of the side streets. "You're here for Lily, not to relive seven-year-old might-have-beens." She wasn't that carefree young woman Jude had once known. Her two years with Shane had changed her. Made her more cautious and unable to trust her own judgment.

A right turn one block later had her searching for the bed-and-breakfast where she would be staying. According to Lily, Granger House Inn was a historic home owned by another of Jude's four brothers and his wife. Fortunately, she'd never met this brother, so there'd be no need for explanations. Yet.

She eased her truck to a stop in front of an impressive sea-foam-green Victorian home with loads of intricate millwork and a gracious front porch. Since Lily's SUV was parked in the drive, this had to be the place.

Kayla turned off the ignition, stepped out of her vehicle and stretched as she drew in a deep breath of mountain air. The clouds had disappeared, leaving a beautiful autumn day in their wake.

She moved up the walk, onto the porch and rang the bell.

A few moments later, Lily swung the

antique-oak-and-leaded-glass door wide. Her long reddish-blond hair was pulled back in a ponytail and her smile was wide. "Kayla!" She hugged her. "I'm so glad you're here."

"Me, too." It did her heart good to see her friend so happy. In recent years, Lily had endured some tough times. Yet, through it all, she'd clung to her faith. And now she'd found a man who shared that faith and recognized Lily for the special woman she was.

Kayla could only hope to be so fortunate.

Lily released her. "Where's your stuff?"

"In the truck."

"Well, let's get you unpacked because I have something I can't wait to show you."

"Such as?" Kayla watched her friend as they started off the porch.

"You'll have to wait and see."

When they returned with her things, another woman stood just inside the door, holding a tiny baby.

"Look who's finally awake." Lily grinned at the child, setting Kayla's suitcase on the wooden floor. "Kayla, this is Carly, my soon-to-be sister-in-law."

"It's nice to meet you, Kayla." The woman had blond curls and smiled warmly, her countenance one of contentment.

"And this little guy here—" Lily reached for the babe's fisted hand "—is Lucas."

Moving closer, Kayla couldn't stop staring. From his downy dark hair to his barely there nose and slow-motion movements… "He's so little. How old is he?"

"Five weeks tomorrow," said Carly.

Kayla could hardly believe that in only four short months, she'd be holding her own baby.

"When are you due?" Carly noted her belly.

"February."

"Do you know what you're having?"

"No, she does not." Lily frowned. "And the suspense is killing me."

Clearing her throat, Kayla regarded her friend. "As a very wise person recently said to me, you'll just have to wait and see."

"Fine." Lily rolled her green eyes and

reached for the suitcase. "Come on, I'll show you your room." She started for the stairs that swept up one side of the parlor.

"Kayla, I put you in the Hayden Room," Carly called after them from the parlor below. "Not only does it have a great view, it's the farthest away from our room down here, so you shouldn't hear the baby."

"I'm sure it'll be perfect. Although, I guess I should get used to hearing a baby's cry." She'd be alone, after all. A truth she sometimes found rather terrifying.

"Ah, don't rush it." The blonde looked lovingly at her child, then back to Kayla. "Enjoy the uninterrupted sleep while you can."

Entering the room at the end of the hall, Lily set the suitcase on the plush gray carpet. "What do you think?"

Kayla moved behind her. "This is gorgeous." From the magnificent view through antique glass to the four-poster queen bed with luxurious bedding...

"Check out the claw-foot tub in the bath-room." Lily nodded in the general direction.

Dropping her hanging clothes and over-night case onto the antique settee, Kayla hurried into the adjoining bathroom with its black-and-white mosaic floor, white beadboard wainscoting and, yes, a claw-foot tub.

"Lily, I may never want to leave this place."

Her friend appeared in the doorway. "Are you referring to your room or Ouray?"

"My room. Though Ouray is pretty in-viting, too."

"I'm glad to hear you say that." Turn-ing, a grinning Lily moved back into the bedroom.

As if Kayla wouldn't follow. "Why?"

Lily crossed to the clothes Kayla had left on the settee and picked them up. "Because I have a proposition for you." She opened the door of the small closet and hung them on the rod.

"What kind of proposition?" Kayla eased

onto the side of the bed, her fingers digging into the softness.

"Are you familiar with the old Congress Hotel?"

"White wooden structure on the other side of town?"

"That's the one."

"I think I went inside it once. As I recall, it had some pretty cool features."

"Yes, it does." Lily met her gaze. "Which is only part of the reason I bought it."

Kayla's eyes went wide. "You bought it? What kind of shape is it in? I mean, it wasn't that great seven years ago."

"And it's been closed up for at least the last five, so I'm sure it's even worse than you remember."

"Yet you bought it?"

"Kayla, I have fallen in love with Ouray. It's my home. And that hotel is a part of this town's history. A history that needs to be preserved for future generations. I want to restore it to its former glory."

"*You're* going to restore it?" While Kayla had no doubt that Lily could afford such a venture, she couldn't quite picture her wealthy friend wielding a hammer, let alone refinishing floors.

"Not me personally. I'm going to hire someone to do the work."

"Okay, so what does that have to do with me? You want me to help you find a general contractor?"

"Sort of." Looking rather sheepish, Lily sat down next to her. "I'd like *you* to be that contractor."

"Lily, a restoration like that could take months. Maybe years."

"I'm aware of that. And I know the baby is coming and everything, but you know historical renovations better than anyone. I mean, you've been doing them for years."

"Lily, I've never been a general contractor before."

"You didn't have the title, but you certainly had all the duties. That's why you always talked about starting your own business." Lily lifted a shoulder. "Even contemplated doing it somewhere other than Denver."

Lily was the only person in this world Kayla would have shared that with.

"This could give you that fresh start you've been looking for. An opportunity to view life from a different angle. I mean, just look at how Ouray has changed my life."

It all sounded wonderful. Too good to be true. But after seeing Jude…

Kayla eyed her friend. "You've put a lot of thought into this, haven't you?"

The corners of Lily's mouth lifted. "Been running this conversation through my head for weeks."

"Seriously? You have a wedding to plan and you're dwelling on a conversation with me?"

"I wouldn't call it dwelling. More like carefully calculating so I'm sure to play up all the right points."

Where would she be if God hadn't brought this woman into her life? She nudged Lily with her elbow. "Have I ever told you how much I love you?"

"Sweetie, you're the sister I never had."

"If that's the case, then you're the annoying sister."

"A distinction I will wear proudly." Lily paused, her expression turning serious. "So, what do you say?"

"Let me see the place first. *After* I put my feet up for a few and grab a snack."

"You do look a little tired." Bottom lip pooched out, Lily reached for her hand. "And here I am, pushing you to do all sorts of stuff. I'm sorry."

Kayla set her free hand atop Lily's. "You're just excited, that's all."

"Still, that doesn't give me the right to be rude." Her friend stood. "You take all the time you need. Though I should tell you that Carly just made an apple crisp that is to die for."

"Ah, that's what I smelled downstairs. Made my stomach growl."

"That happens when you're eating for two." Lily moved toward the door. "I'll see you in a bit." She reached for the knob and started to pull it closed.

"Lily?" Kayla rested her back against the

plethora of pillows and stretched her legs out on the bed.

"Yes?"

She grabbed a throw pillow, hugging it against her chest. "Don't expect me to give you an answer right away. I'll have to think on this one awhile."

Lily grinned. "I know you will. And I'll be praying that God will lead us both to the right decision."

Chapter Two

Jude eased his truck into the parking spot next to Lily's SUV, still trying to get Kayla out of his mind. Between last night's conversation with his father and seeing her today, he was wound up tighter than a two-dollar watch.

God, I sure wish I knew what You're trying to teach me. Because whatever it was, he'd just as soon learn it and move on.

This might be a good night to lock himself in his shop and sort through his thoughts while he turned some spindles. That always seemed to relax him.

Killing the engine, he stared at the old Congress Hotel. The three-story wooden structure that had once been labeled "the finest on the Western Slope" seemed to be disintegrating before his eyes. The white paint was either peeling or completely gone, the open veranda on the second floor that extended over the sidewalk sagged and much of the trim appeared damaged by the elements and countless years of neglect. He hated to see it. Though its restoration would be a major undertaking for anyone.

Noting that one of the two doors on the front of the building stood open, he climbed out, eager to learn what Lily was up to.

Still wearing his uniform—a black tactical shirt and gray cargo pants—he continued across the sidewalk and up the concrete steps until he stood on the vintage wooden floors that graced the hotel's lobby. With its tin ceiling and antique furnishings, it felt as though he'd stepped into another place in time.

The sun had already dipped behind Twin Peaks along the town's western edge, and the remaining daylight struggled to make its way through the hazy stained-glass-rimmed windows along the front.

"Lily?" He glanced up the staircase to his left before continuing past the ornately carved registration desk. Hearing sounds coming from the dining room, he moved in that direction.

"Lil—" The sight of Kayla standing on a ladder stopped him in his tracks and sent his mind racing back to their first meeting. They'd both been hired by a local contractor to help with the restoration of one of the largest Victorian homes in town. She'd been standing on a ladder that day, too. And he'd been smitten the first moment he saw her.

Hauling his traitorous mind back to the present, he cleared his throat. "Do you think it's wise for you to be up there in your condition?"

She shot him an annoyed look before returning her focus to the peeling wallpaper. "Trust me, I was doing this long before I was in this *condition*."

"True, but your center of equilibrium is

different now. What if you were to fall? What would your husband say?"

Using what looked like a pocketknife, she carefully pried another sliver of paper away from the plaster. "I doubt he'd care."

Confused, he took a step closer and set a hand on the ladder, just in case. "Why do you say that?"

She closed the knife, tucked it into the pocket of her jeans and stepped down. "Because he's dead."

He stood there, blinking, feeling as though someone had just hit him with a left hook. Her husband was dead? He glanced at her swollen belly. Leaving Kayla to raise their child alone. "I—I'm sorry."

"Don't be." She collapsed the ladder and leaned it against the wall. "My baby and I are doing just fine."

"Sorry, I took so long." Lily breezed into the room then, stirring up the stale air. "Jude, I'm glad you're here." She looked from him to her friend. "Kayla, this is Noah's brother Jude. He specializes in historic millwork reproduction."

He waited to see what Kayla would do. Would she tell Lily that they already knew each other? That they'd fallen in love? Or at least he had. Something that, apparently, hadn't been reciprocated.

Kayla's gaze drifted to his. "Historic millwork?" He thought he saw a hint of a smile. "So, you're not just a police officer." Why did that seem to please her? And why did her reaction bolster him?

"No, he is not," Lily responded before he had a chance. "I've seen his work, and he's quite talented. He can replicate almost anything, and you would never know it wasn't an original." Turning, she sent him a grin. "Which is why I asked you to meet me here."

He shoved his hands into the pockets of his cargo pants. "I'd be lying if I said I wasn't curious."

"I want to restore this building. The hotel, restaurant, perhaps—" she strode to the center of the room "—and I can just envision this dining room being used for wedding receptions and parties…"

His suspicions had been right. Scanning the decrepit dining room with its water-stained wallpaper and warped wooden floorboards, he could see Lily's vision, but—

"You're looking at a lot of work, Lily, and that's going to translate to money." He crossed to stand beside her. "This room alone looks as though it has a fair amount of water damage. I don't know where the water came from, but if it was overhead, then the damage is likely worse on the two upper floors."

She eyed him matter-of-factly. "I've already seen it. And yes, it is. But if someone doesn't come in here and do something soon, things will continue to deteriorate, and it'll cost even more." She sent him a pleading look. "Jude, Ouray has blessed me in so many ways. If I can help save a part of its history, then I don't care what it costs."

He smiled down at the likable woman who had more money than he could ever fathom. "Even if you weren't marrying my brother, there's no way I could say no to that. Just tell me what you want me to do."

"There's lot of damaged millwork throughout the building. I'd like you to replicate it and oversee the installation."

"Sure, I can do that. Who's your contractor?"

"I'm not certain yet." Lily strolled toward Kayla. "However, my sweet friend here has worked as a house flipper for a number of years."

"I work *for* a house flipper." Kayla was quick to correct.

"He purchases the homes, but you're the one who oversees all of his projects. And you do a fair amount of the work yourself." Taking Kayla by the arm, Lily again faced Jude. "Since her specialty is historic homes, I'm hoping she'll agree to act as general contractor for me."

Whoa, what? Kayla as general contractor? That meant they'd be working together again. And while he trusted Lily's judgment...

He scraped his boot across the worn

floorboards. Man, why had he been so quick to say yes?

His only hope now was that Kayla would say no. Because from the sound of things, she already had a job. Sure, she and Lily were friends, but why would she give up that job and move to Ouray for one project? Especially when she was pregnant.

His gaze drifted across the room to the dark-haired beauty. Then again, she was used to a more itinerant lifestyle. Perhaps, now that her husband was gone, she'd decided she'd been in one place for too long.

Pink tinged Kayla's cheeks. "Lily, I told you I'd think about it."

"I know you did. So let's go have a look at the rest of the place." Lily motioned for them to follow her as she started back into the lobby. "Perhaps that will help convince you."

Or scare her away.

They were almost to the stairway when Lily's phone rang. She looked at the screen. "Sorry, guys, I need to take this." Aiming for the front door, she added, "I shouldn't be long."

A silent moment passed before Kayla turned to him. "I'm relieved to hear you're still doing your woodworking." She lifted a shoulder. "After seeing you at the park, I was afraid you'd given it up in favor of police work."

"No way. That was just to tide me over until I could make a living with the wood-working. Now I'm planning on giving up the day job so I can devote all my time to millwork." Why had he told her all that? Even if he wasn't faced with the possibility of breaking his father's heart, it was none of her business.

"Wow, that's great." She smiled. "I've often thought about starting my own flipping business. Only historic homes, though." She absently smoothed a hand over her belly. "Of course, now I have to look at the bigger picture and think about how my decisions will affect others."

He inched closer. "Speaking of decisions, you're not really considering taking Lily up on her offer, are you?"

Her brow lifted. "Why shouldn't I? There's nothing tying me to Denver."

He searched her dark eyes. So much for settling down. Evidently, the wanderer in her still couldn't stand the thought of being stuck in one place for too long.

Good thing he hadn't asked her to stay all those years ago. No matter how badly he'd wanted to.

"Or are you afraid the job might be too much for a woman in my *condition*?" Her words flew all over him.

Maybe he had stepped in it with that comment. Yet while his mother had raised him and his brothers to be gentlemen, she'd also been an example of just how capable women could be. Something Kayla knew good and well, having spent a fair amount of time with the woman.

Standing toe-to-toe with her, he said, "I think you know me better than that." For a second he thought he saw her wince.

Then she perched her hands on the backs of her hips and glared up at him. "Do I?"

"You would if you'd stuck around." Realizing what he'd said, he jammed a hand through his hair and turned away. He must be more stressed than he thought. He was talking like a crazy man.

Thankfully, Lily whisked past him. "We're running out of daylight, so we need to hurry if we're going to manage even a cursory look."

As he followed the two women up the broad staircase, he couldn't help wondering what he'd gotten himself into.

Kayla stared out the window of Lily's SUV, eyeing the lights of Main Street on the way back to Granger House Inn. *You would if you'd stuck around.*

Again, Jude's words played through her head, confusing her and messing with her already tired mind. Had he wanted her to stay all those years ago?

Her eyes briefly fell closed. Foolish. She'd given him every opportunity in the world to ask her to stay and he hadn't. Despite all of her comments about loving Ouray and how it felt like a good place to call home, he'd let her drive away with her parents without so much as a wish that she would stay.

None of that mattered now anyway. He was the one who'd deemed their relationship over. She'd moved on with her life. Gotten married. She had a baby on the way, and Lily had offered her an incredible opportunity.

What was her problem then? Why was she finding it so difficult to say yes? Like she'd told Jude, there was nothing tying her to Denver. The house she'd shared with Shane had sold months ago, what little stuff she had was in storage and since she'd been living at Lily's there was no lease to worry about. All she had was her job. One she was already considering leaving to start her own company. Throw in the fact that Ouray was the one place she'd always dreamed of settling down…

Except you'd dreamed of settling down with Jude.

She blew out a breath, fogging up the window. That was seven years ago. She'd been twenty-one and still traveling from place to place with her parents in an RV. Of course she'd wanted to settle down. She'd spent her entire life roaming. She'd wanted a place to call home. To make friendships that lasted more than six months and have the opportunity to fall in love and start a family.

Things she'd ultimately achieved in Denver. Aside from her friendship with Lily, though, her life wasn't the fairy tale she'd envisioned. Instead, she'd found herself perpetually walking on eggshells, always hoping and praying Shane would come home sober. When he did, he could be the most charming person in the world. But if he didn't...

Now she had a baby to think about. What if she made the wrong decision and messed up her child's life the way she had hers?

"You're awful quiet over there." Lily glanced at her across the center console.

Darkness had fallen over Ouray, so Kayla couldn't say she was taking in the view. "Just thinking."

"In that case, I have something else for you to ponder."

"As if I need more." Twisting, she feigned annoyance.

"Sorry." Lily stared straight ahead, her brow puckering. "That was my Realtor who called earlier." Making a right turn, she glanced Kayla's way. "We received a full-price offer on the house today."

She straightened. "Full-price? That's excellent."

"It is." Lily let go a sigh. "However, it also means that you're going to have to find another place to live."

"Lily, you were doing me a favor, remember?" And while Kayla had been looking, she had yet to find anything that felt like home. "We knew this was inevitable."

"I know, but..." Her friend hesitated.

"I'm not trying to pressure you or anything, but I should let you know that I've already spoken with Andrew and Carly and if you do decide to stay in Ouray, you can live in Livie's House, the little folk Victorian next door to Granger House Inn. It belonged to Andrew and Jude's grandmother, but now it's used as an extension of the bed-and-breakfast. You'd have the whole house to yourself."

She remembered that house. She and Jude used to stop by to play cards with his grandmother, a sweet lady who made some of the best chocolate chip cookies Kayla had ever tasted.

"I will take that into consideration." Again, she stared outside. *God, You're trying to tell me something, aren't You?*

She was still wrestling with herself when they eased to a stop in front of Granger House Inn.

"Lily, there's something I need to share with you."

Unfastening her seat belt, her friend looked concerned. "What is it, sweetie?"

"You know how I told you about me and my parents spending time in Ouray?"

"How could I forget? Your glowing accounts were what made me decide to come here."

"Well..." Kayla picked at her barely there fingernails. "What I failed to tell you is that, during those six months, I fell in love. With Jude Stephens."

Lily's jaw dropped. "You're kidding me."

She'd never seen her friend's eyes so big. "I wish I were."

The lights of the dashboard glowed as Lily turned in her leather seat. "That is crazy. I mean, what is the likelihood that... Wait, do you still love him?"

"Lily, I was married to another man."

"Okay." Lily brushed a stray hair away from her face. "Maybe *love* wasn't the right word. But do you still have feelings for him?"

Kayla had feelings all right. A jumbled concoction of them, most of which were probably brought on by the child growing inside of her. She shrugged. "He was my first love, so, yeah, it was kind of exciting to see him again."

"He's not married, you know." Lily grinned with what Kayla was sure was matchmaking glee. "How do you think he felt about seeing you?"

"That's easy. Stunned."

"Stunned?"

"Of course he was. I mean, we tried to stay in touch, but you know how that goes." Especially when one person says they're done and the other loses her phone, along with every contact she had stored in it. "He had no idea I was your matron of honor." She shook her head. "And that's my fault for not saying something to you as soon as you told me you were marrying Noah."

"Wait, have you met Noah?"

"No, he was on the rodeo circuit when I lived here. And Andrew was living in Denver. The middle brother—"

"Matt?"

"Yeah, he wasn't around either. But I spent a lot of time at their ranch, so I got to know Daniel and their mom and dad. I loved Mona."

Lily's countenance fell. "I hate to tell you this, Kayla, but she passed away a few years ago."

Tears pricked the backs of Kayla's eyes. Tilting her head upward, she tried to blink them away. Mona was the one person she was really looking forward to seeing again. Because if anyone could make sense of Kayla's crazy life, it was Jude's mother. "How?"

"Cancer."

The same stupid disease that had taken her father. She pressed her back against the seat. "That stinks."

"Yes, it does. Noah's told me a lot about her. I wish I'd had the opportunity to meet her."

Kayla rolled her head to stare at her friend. "She would have loved you, Lily."

"You think so?"

"I know so. Mona loved everyone."

Lily wrinkled her nose. "I suppose I should warn you that Clint has a girlfriend. Hillary Ward-Thompson. She's very sweet."

"How do the guys feel about that?" If there was one thing she knew for certain, it was that the Stephens' boys were crazy about their mother.

"They're okay with it. Probably because she and Clint were old friends and it's been a very slow growing relationship. Noah says she's good at keeping his father in line."

They both chuckled.

"I seem to recall Clint being a bit of handful," added Kayla.

Sobering, Lily said, "I know you have a lot of other things to consider, but is Jude part of the reason you're having a hard time making a decision?"

"Honestly, I'm too tired to think. Plus, it's only been, what, three, four hours since you sprang this on me? I thought we'd be talking about wedding stuff, not renovations."

"Don't worry, there will be plenty of wedding stuff."

"I hope so, because I'm looking forward to all those girlie things. For now, though—" Kayla unhooked her seat belt "—I think I just need some dinner and a good night's rest." One that was, hopefully, not interrupted by a dangerously handsome police officer and images of what might have been.

Chapter Three

Jude breathed in the calming aroma of sawdust while the hum of his lathe provided the white noise that usually relaxed him. Tonight, though, he was neither calm nor relaxed.

He removed the freshly turned spindle from the machine, ran a hand over the smooth wood grain before setting it aside, then put another block of wood in its place. He needed to escape reality for a while and take some time to collect his thoughts. He hadn't felt this torn, this discombobulated since…since the day his mother died.

He wished she was here now to listen

and help him sort through the chaos banging around inside of him.

He had already made his decision to resign from the police department when his father approached him about taking over the cattle business. The man was nothing if not proud. Proud of his family and the business he'd worked hard to build. How could Jude tell him he wasn't interested? Dad wasn't getting any younger, after all. It was only natural he'd want to step aside, assured that his legacy would live on.

And then there was Kayla. Widowed, pregnant and back in Ouray for Noah's wedding. Longer, if she agreed to take on Lily's hotel project.

Shaking his head, he set the lathe to spinning. He quickly shaved off the corners of the wood with his roughing gouge, leaving him with a plain cylinder.

Perhaps what irked him the most was his reaction to seeing her. She was the one who'd broken off all contact with him, yet all he could think about were the good times they'd had when she was here. Working together by day, long talks at night. They'd been practically inseparable.

Some weeks, Kayla spent more time at the ranch than she did with her own parents. They'd shared their hopes and dreams, went to church together and had a mutual respect for Ouray's history, particularly the architecture. Over 70 percent of the town's Victorian-era structures were still in use today. Everything from Queen Anne style to Italianate to Colonial Revival, Craftsman and more. And during Kayla's time here, the two of them had analyzed each and every one, verbally renovating those that had fallen into disrepair and noting the finer points of those that had been restored. Even one he'd thought would make the perfect house for the two of them to raise a family.

He swapped his gouge for a chisel. No, he'd never met anyone quite like Kayla, either before or since. He supposed that made her one of a kind. Problem with that was that every other woman paled in comparison.

What would he do if Kayla decided to stay? Was he man enough to work alongside her again, knowing they would never be anything more than friends? If they were even that after the way they butted heads today.

A sudden burst of cool evening air had him glancing at the door to see Noah coming toward him.

Nudging his cowboy hat back a notch, his brother surveyed the space. "Figured I'd find you here." His gaze shifted to Jude, then the lathe. "You working or hiding?"

Jude slid his goggles to the top of his head. "You know what they say about killing two birds with one stone."

"Who or what are you hiding from then?" Noah picked up a spindle and studied it.

"Dad."

His brother paused. "What did the old man do now?"

"Has he said anything to you about retiring?"

Noah thought for a moment, then shook his head. "No, I don't believe so."

"You're sure?"

"I think I would have remembered that. Why?"

The knot in Jude's stomach tightened. Dad talked to Noah about everything. But if he hadn't mentioned Jude taking over the cattle business, perhaps Jude shouldn't bring it up either.

How was Jude going to dig his way out of this? "I was just curious, that's all. He is getting older..."

"Old or not, Dad's too ornery to retire." Noah returned the spindle to the pile. "Besides, who'd run the ranch if he did?" His dark gaze narrowed on Jude. "Unless you're wanting to take over."

"No way. I—"

"Jude, I was hoping you'd be in here."

He looked in the direction of the door to see Lily moving toward him with purposeful steps. A smile lit her face when she spotted Noah.

"Hi, honey." Wading through a pile of wood chips, she pushed up on the toes of her boots and gave her fiancé a brief kiss. "Where are the kids?"

"Watching TV with Dad." Their father had grown quite fond of Lily's children, ten-year-old Colton and seven-year-old Piper. And like his other two nieces and nephew, they seemed to bring out the best in the old man.

She turned her attention back to Jude and let go a sigh, her petite shoulders sagging. "Kayla told me about the two of you. I hope you don't think I was trying to pull one over on you. I had no idea you knew each other."

"It's all right, Lily." He sent her a reassuring smile.

"Are you still going to be all right with everything? After all, seeing someone you cared about after such a long time can be quite a shock. And then with her being pregnant and all."

"Whoa...time-out." Noah formed a T with his hands. He looked at Lily. "Kayla is your matron of honor?"

"Yes."

Still confused, Noah faced Jude. "And you know her?"

"*Knew* her. It was a long time ago."

Lily nodded. "Seven years." Her comment had Jude wondering what else Kayla had told her.

Noah crossed his arms over his chest. "Just how well did you know her?"

"Jude, we got a problem." Dad blew into the building.

Got that right. Jude might need to start locking the door.

"Oh." The old man's steps slowed when he spotted Noah and Lily. "Sorry, didn't know you had company."

"It's all right, Dad." Noah turned. "We were just discussing Lily's matron of honor, Kayla."

"Kayla?" Their father's brow creased. "Jude, you knew a—"

"Yeah. It's her."

"The one that got away?" Why had Dad felt the need to add that?

"Got away?" Arms still crossed, Noah puffed out his chest all big-brother-like. "Is there something else you'd care to tell me?"

Lips pressed tightly together, Jude shook his head. "Nope."

"You were head over heels for that one." Dad rubbed the stubble lining his chin. "Never could figure out why you didn't ask her to marry you."

Noah and Lily exchanged a look.

"I was twenty-two years old. I didn't know what I wanted." *Yes, you did. You wanted Kayla.* But given his uncertainty about what he'd wanted to do with his life, not to mention her need to roam... "What's the problem, Dad?"

The old man's brows shot up. "Problem?"

"When you came in here, you said we had a problem."

"Oh, that. Sheriff's department called. Said we got a couple of cows wandering around on the county road."

We? Jude didn't own any cows. And he'd prefer to keep it that way.

"Fence must be down somewhere." Dad shoved his hands into the pockets of his Carhartt jacket. "The faster we get it taken care of, the better off we'll be."

"Need me to help?" said Noah.

"No, you got your hands full with the rodeo school."

Jude could hardly believe his ears. Noah had always helped them. Now that the rodeo school had opened, he was too busy? Meanwhile, Dad still thought Jude's wood-working was only a hobby. He shook his head.

"Utility vehicle is waiting outside." The old man started toward the door. "Grab a jacket and we'll head out."

"I'd better check on the kids." Lily brushed past Jude and followed his father out the door.

Jude's breathing grew quicker. He felt his nostrils flare. He did not want to fix any fence. He didn't want any cows. He wanted to be in his shop, working on *his* business, following *his* dreams. To do that, though, he'd have to break the news to his father. See the hurt and disappointment in his eyes.

And he didn't have the strength for that tonight.

* * *

The sun was shining and the air was crisp when Kayla emerged from Granger House Inn the next morning. Perfect weather for a walk. And after the breakfast she'd just eaten, she might need a long one. Carly had prepared a delectable spread of home-made muffins, ham-and-cheese quiche, bacon, sausage, biscuits…and Kayla had sampled it all.

She rubbed her tummy. "Don't get too used to that, little one. Mommy can't afford to eat like that all the time." She'd never be able to fit into her clothes.

After twisting her hair into a single braid, she continued down the steps of the sprawling porch and shoved her hands into the pockets of her denim overalls, noting the pale gray folk Victorian house next door. With its white trim, flower boxes and cozy porch, it reminded her of a quaint cottage instead of the run-of-the-mill older home it had been the last time she'd seen it. And she'd get to live there if she decided to stay.

Which led her to this morning's mission. Revisiting the old Congress Hotel. Between the dim lighting last night and her rapidly dwindling energy, Kayla owed it to herself and her friend to take another look at what the project might entail before making any decisions. When Kayla had texted earlier, Lily had responded that she'd have the Realtor, who lived nearby and still kept an extra key for occasions such as this, unlock the door.

While Kayla had slept well last night, she'd awoken early, her mind ablaze with the options that lay before her. If she stayed in Denver, she'd have to find a new place to live right away, which meant she'd probably have to settle for something less than perfect and then move again within a year. Unless she was able to find an older home she could flip at some point. Still, having a house like that baby-ready in four months would be a challenge even if she wasn't pregnant. And, of course, any notions of starting her own business would have to wait until after the baby came and she'd settled into motherhood.

Lifting her gaze, she took in the rustic beauty of the conifer-dotted redstone cliffs at the town's northeastern edge. Ouray was a unique beauty. Majestic and awe-inspiring, yet comfortable. It had that welcoming vibe that invited a person to stick around for a while. She'd felt it when she was twenty-one, and now, Lily had presented her with the perfect opportunity to linger.

Overseeing a job as big as the Congress Hotel would boost Kayla's career to another level, perhaps giving her recognition she'd never gain doing homes. She'd also have a house provided for her and a boss she would desperately miss if she went back to Denver.

But then there was Jude. For the life of her, she couldn't figure out why he was such a sticking point. Their relationship was over long ago. She'd loved her husband and had determined to stay with him for better or for worse.

She focused on the sidewalk. Though

sometimes, when things were at their worst, she'd allow her mind to wander back to a time when she didn't have a care in the world. And there was a man at her side who treated her like a queen.

She squeezed her eyes shut. *Forgive me, Lord. I know it was wrong of me to think of Jude when I was married to Shane. Even if they were only innocent thoughts of feeling safe and protected. Forgive me.*

Looking up, she eyed a couple of aspens bearing a mixture of green and gold leaves. By this time next week, the trees were apt to be completely golden, creating a perfect backdrop for Lily's wedding photos.

The two of them would be making a run to Grand Junction in a couple of hours to pick up their dresses. Lord willing, Kayla wouldn't grow much more before next week. Though, considering the breakfast she just ate, she hoped the seamstress left a little extra room in hers.

Nonetheless, that was precisely the type of thing she had been looking forward to most this week. Aside from Lily, Kayla didn't have many friends, making girl time a rarity—and almost nonexistent since Lily had been gone.

Sounds like another good reason to take Lily up on her offer.

She continued across Main Street and straight ahead to the hotel. From farther away, it didn't look so bad. But the closer she got...

Yeah, the outside was in pretty bad shape. Far more than paint alone could remedy. It was a cool-looking building, though. It had an Old West flavor with a touch of Italianate.

The door was unlocked, as promised, and Kayla left it open when she went inside, hoping some fresh air might filter into the musty space. Since she'd already gotten a pretty good look at the main floor, she headed upstairs.

Though carpeted, the steps seemed solid, so that was a plus. However, depending on the wood, they might want to consider replacing the tattered carpet with a runner, leaving the wood exposed at the edges, the way they would have when the hotel was built.

Reaching the top, she continued across the hall and opened a solid wood door. Inside was a smaller-than-small guest room with an iron bed frame and not much else, except for a pile of clutter in the corner that had her doing a double take. Had something just moved?

Taking a step back, she narrowed her gaze as a rat bolted from the heap.

Kayla screamed and rushed into the hall, slamming the door closed behind her. That's when she heard the sound of footsteps pounding up the stairs.

Her heart thudded wildly. She looked up and down the hall. There was nowhere to hide except for another room. What if it had rats, too?

"Kayla?" Jude's panic-stricken face came into view as he neared the top of the stairs.

"Jude? What are you—"

"I heard you scream." He moved toward her, his dark gaze probing. "Are you all right?"

She struggled to catch her breath. "I—I

did scream, didn't I?" She slumped against the water-stained wallpapered wall.

He was beside her now. "What happened?" Concern creased his brow.

With a final gasp, she straightened but refused to look at him. "There was a pile of junk in there, and a rat ran out of it."

"A rat?"

She nodded.

"Wait a minute. Don't you work on old houses all the time?"

"Yes." She lifted a shoulder. "He startled me, that's all."

"That's all?" Hands perched low on his denim-clad hips, he started to pace. "You scared me half to death."

"You? Why were you scared?"

He faced her again. "Bloodcurdling screams have a way of doing that."

Heat crept into her cheeks. "Sorry about that. I… Wait, why were you here in the first place?"

"I wanted to look at the place in the daylight. I saw the door was open…"

"And you couldn't have let me know you were here?"

"I'd barely walked in when you screamed."

"Oh." She glanced at the crusty blue-green carpet on the floor. Why did he have to show up now? Acting like a white knight, no less, hurrying to her rescue. "Well, I'm fine, so you're free to go about your business."

"My business is here. We may as well join forces and check the place out together." The corners of his mouth lifted. "In case there are any more rats."

She glared at him. "For the record, I usually carry a baseball bat when I'm at my job sites. Just in case."

"Ever used it?"

"A couple of times."

His lip curled. "Ew."

"Yeah, it wasn't pretty." She absently played with her braid. "But seriously, I'm fine. You just go check out whatever it was you came to see."

He studied her for a long moment. "Are you sure you shouldn't go lie down or put your feet up or something? You had quite a scare."

Did he really just say that? "I'm sorry, but who are you to tell me what to do?"

"I'm not trying to tell you what to do, I'm simply trying to make sure your baby is safe."

She crossed her arms over her chest. "You're a doctor now?"

"No, but—"

"And when was the last time you were pregnant?"

"All right, that's it. I've had enough of you treating me like I'm some sort of male chauvinist pig. Can't a guy just be concerned?"

Not when he's too chivalrous for my own good. "Not if he keeps trying to tell me what to do." Her days of being bullied were over.

"Since when have I tried telling you what to do?"

"You just told me to lie down and put my feet up." She took a step closer, her father's Irish temper getting the best of her. "So just to make things clear, not only am I *not* going to put my feet up, I'm going to take Lily up on her offer and turn this hotel into the greatest thing Ouray has ever seen."

Chapter Four

What had she done?

From the passenger seat of Lily's luxury SUV, Kayla studied the mesas in the distance as they approached Grand Junction. Why had she let Jude get to her like that?

She straightened. Because after Shane's death, she'd promised herself that she would always stand her ground and never again allow herself to be intimidated by another person. But instead of behaving rationally, she'd dug her heels in and made a snap decision before she'd even finished looking at the building.

A decision she was now second-guessing. Renovating the Congress Hotel would be a major undertaking for even the most experienced contractor, let alone a pregnant widow plagued with self-doubt. Never mind the fact that she'd be having a baby in four months, followed by weeks of recovery. Between now and then, there would be permits to obtain, crews to hire, furniture would need to be removed...and that was all before a hammer could be swung. Throw in Thanksgiving, Christmas and New Year's to slow things down, and they'd have barely begun by the time the baby arrived. How would she oversee things then?

Yet, in the nearly two hours since she and Lily had left Ouray, all they'd talked about was the wedding, a pleasure Kayla had been looking forward to for weeks. But the subject of the hotel was one she could no longer avoid. Not after opening her big mouth in front of Jude.

Kayla studied the woman in the driver's seat, the one who'd offered her the opportunity of a lifetime. Lily had way too much faith in her. What if Kayla did something wrong? Cost her friend even more money? Or worse, let Lily down?

The vehicle slowed, and Kayla eyed the city limit sign. And to think, she used to be so bold. Approaching life and all it offered with such confidence. But thanks to her bad choices, that girl no longer existed.

She cleared her throat. "So…about the hotel project."

Lily glanced her way, her expectant smile instantaneous. "Have you made a decision?"

"Um…have you thought this through, Lily? Like I said, it may be a month or more before anyone could even get started. By then we'll be rolling into the holidays, and shortly after that the baby will be here."

"Something I can hardly wait for." Her green eyes fixed on the road ahead, Lily beamed like a proud aunt. And while they weren't related by blood, Lily was the closest thing Kayla's child would have to an aunt.

"You realize this baby's arrival is likely

to keep me away from the job site for several weeks while I recover, right? I mean, I might be able to pop in occasionally, but that's it."

Lily eased onto a side street, her brow furrowing. "You don't want to do it, do you?"

"It's not that I don't want to. Any other time I'd kill for a job like this. I'd be working for you. Best boss ever. But I don't want to disappoint you."

Lily reached for Kayla's hand. "Sweetie, I considered everything you mentioned before I asked you to be my contractor. It's not like I have a deadline for this project. I just want to see the hotel brought back to life, because right now it's a sad piece of Ouray's history that's slowly going away."

Kayla couldn't argue with that. Back when she and Jude used to walk the town, studying the older buildings, he'd told her that the Congress Hotel had been an integral part of Ouray. Built in the early 1890s, it survived the depression years of the silver crisis that struck in 1893, thrived during the Gold Rush later in the decade and carried Ouray into the twentieth century. Kayla didn't want to see it vanish either. Not when it still had so much potential.

Lily pulled into a small parking lot, and Kayla glanced at the brick building in front of them as they came to a stop. Discussion of the hotel would have to wait. This appointment was about Lily and her special day.

"I can't wait to see your dress."

"Mine?" Her friend killed the engine. "You haven't even seen yours yet."

"No." Kayla had simply sent her measurements. "But I trust your judgment."

Lily reached for her door, then paused, looking at Kayla over her shoulder. "Just like I trust yours."

While Kayla knew what her friend was saying, there was a lot of difference between a historic building and a bridesmaid dress.

Outside the vehicle, the sun touched her skin, warming her as the two made their way inside the shop. The owner, a well-dressed silver-haired woman Kayla guessed to be in her sixties, promptly greeted them.

"Lily, I'm so glad to see you again." The woman enveloped Lily in a brief hug.

"Monique, this is Kayla, my matron of honor."

Smiling, Monique clasped her hands against her ample chest. "Kayla, you are even more beautiful than Lily said you were." Her gaze lowered. "And that little girl growing inside of you will be just as lovely as her mother."

Kayla laid a hand atop her belly. "Oh, I don't know what I'm having."

The woman gasped, touching the tips of her fingers to her mouth. "I'm sorry, I've given it away." She winked at Lily then, wagging a finger. "But I am never wrong." With that, she turned and sashayed toward the U-shaped counter in the center of the space.

Kayla and Lily exchanged a look before Lily shrugged and followed Monique.

"Would either of you care for a snack before we get started?" Monique held out a silver tray adorned with hors d'oeuvres and miniature cupcakes.

Considering it was almost two and Kayla hadn't had anything since breakfast, she helped herself to a finger sandwich while Lily went for a cupcake.

"If you ladies will excuse me for one moment." Monique set the tray on the counter before disappearing into a back room.

Nibbling on her chicken salad sandwich, Kayla took in the array of dresses on display in the upscale shop. Princess gowns, strapless gowns, mermaid and sheath dresses. Some were covered in lace while others sparkled with jewels. Good thing she'd ditched her overalls for a pair of black yoga pants and a short-sleeved tunic top. Not exactly the height of fashion, but at least she didn't look like a construction worker.

Sandwich devoured, she returned for a cupcake. She recalled the joy of choosing the perfect dress for her wedding. If only the memories of her marriage were as pleasurable. Shortly after Shane's death, she'd opted to donate her gown to Goodwill, praying it might serve as a sweet remembrance for the next person who wore it.

"Come look at this, Kayla."

She joined Lily in a far corner of the shop where numerous wedding photos adorned a brick wall.

"I love the rustic arbor in this photo." Lily pointed.

"That is pretty." Kayla eyed the simple squared arch made of cedar. "Is that what you're planning to have?"

"No." Her friend faced her. "All the planner had to offer was one that was painted white. I wanted something with character. You know, that has that rustic feel."

Kayla nodded at the photograph. "Well, that would definitely do the trick." And if they were back in Denver, she could easily create one just like it. But without her power tools or a place to do it…

"Oh, well." Her friend shrugged. "There's not much I can do about it now." She inched closer, a twinkle in her green eyes. "So, I guess you're having a girl."

Kayla scanned the area to make sure Monique was no where in sight. "You don't really believe her, do you?"

"She says she's never wrong."

"There's a first time for everything."

"True. But a little girl would be so much fun. Just think of all the cute—"

"Ladies, I have your dresses ready." Monique waved them toward the dressing rooms.

Kayla waited as Lily slipped into her dress, helped her with the zipper, then stared at her friend. The simple ivory cap-sleeved satin sheath dress was as elegant and understated as the woman wearing it. "Lily, it's perfect."

"You think so?" She glanced at her profile in the mirror, smoothing a hand over the nipped waist.

"It's sophisticated and classic. Just like you."

"Not too much for a rustic wedding?"

"Never."

Lily grinned. "Your turn."

"Okay." Kayla hurried into the next room to don her dress.

A few minutes later, Kayla joined her friend at the mirrors in the main part of the store, feeling somewhat uneasy. Though the long flowing dress with a fitted bodice and off-the-shoulder sleeves exceeded her expectations for a maternity gown, it was a far cry from the jeans and T-shirts she was used to wearing.

A grinning Lily tugged her in front of the mirror. "You look absolutely stunning."

Kayla wasn't sure about that. "It's been a long time since I've worn something so feminine."

"Do you like it?"

She pondered her reflection a moment. "It is flattering." It even camouflaged her baby bump. "And I love the color."

"Me, too." Lily peered at the shop's owner. "Monique and I agreed that plum was the perfect shade for you."

The older woman set to work then, scrutinizing the fit of each of their dresses, making certain they were just so.

Once they'd changed back into their regular clothes, Lily and Kayla grabbed their dresses, said their goodbyes and climbed into Lily's vehicle for the drive back to Ouray.

"I have a confession to make." Kayla eyed her friend as they began to pull out of the parking lot.

"Uh-oh." Lily put on the brakes. "You hate the dress, don't you?"

"No, not at all. There's just something I haven't told you."

Still skeptical, her friend continued down the road. "And that would be…?"

"I kinda already told Jude I was going to accept your job offer."

Knuckles white around the steering wheel, Lily said, "What do you mean, you kind of told him?"

"I got mad when he started trying to tell me what to do."

Stopping at the corner, Lily looked right

then left before making her turn. "Telling you what to do? Like what?"

"When I was at the hotel this morning, something startled me, and I screamed. Jude came rushing to my rescue, then *suggested* I go put my feet up so the baby wouldn't be stressed."

Lily laughed then.

"Why are you laughing?"

"Because I can totally hear Jude saying that. And Noah and Clint… That's the Stephens men for you. Gentlemen to the core, thanks to their mother. Or so I've been told."

"Yeah, well, it gets annoying."

Lily reached across the console to lay a hand on her arm. "Kayla, Jude's not Shane. He wouldn't try to make you do anything you didn't want to do." She glanced her way. "But then, I think you already know that."

Somewhere deep inside, she did. Recent history had her on high alert, though. "I not only refused to put my feet up, I told him I was going to turn the hotel into the greatest thing Ouray had ever seen."

A slow smile split her friend's face. "Does this mean…?"

She nodded. "If you're certain, then I guess so."

"Yay! Now we'll really have something to celebrate tonight."

"What's tonight?"

"We're all having dinner at the ranch. Didn't I tell you?"

"No…" She would have remembered that. And then tried to come up with a way to bow out so she wouldn't have to face Jude again today.

"Hmm. Guess I only thought I told you. The whole family is getting together for dinner tonight, and you're invited, too."

"Sounds like fun." Or not. Now she really wished Jude's mother was still alive. Despite everything, she would have made Kayla feel welcome and right at home. This time, Kayla had to find her own way.

This was one family dinner Jude did not want to attend.

Not that he wasn't used to them. But in the past year and half, they'd added what would soon be three sisters-in-law, three nieces and two nephews to their numbers. And while he mostly enjoyed family gatherings, occasionally he felt left out because he didn't have someone to share his life with.

That feeling had amplified since Kayla's return. And her presence at tonight's supper would likely make things even more challenging.

She's staying in Ouray, buddy, so you'd better get used to it.

A sweet aroma met him as he emerged from the hallway into the living room of the ranch house. "Something smells good."

"That would be pumpkin crunch cake." Armed with pot holders, Matt's wife, Lacie, pulled a baking dish from the oven in the adjoining kitchen.

His other sister-in-law, Carly, cleared a spot on the counter while Dad's girlfriend, Hillary, closed the oven door.

"Well, if it tastes as good as it smells..." He continued toward the wooden dining table where his infant nephew, Lucas, sat quietly in his seat, oblivious to all of the activity. Jude nudged a finger under the baby's fisted hand until he took hold. "How's it going, buddy? You keeping these ladies in line? Where's everyone else?" he tossed over his shoulder.

"Outside." Hillary moved beside him, smiling at Lucas.

He glanced at the woman who'd found a place in all of their hearts. "Dad manning the grill?" Hillary had given it to the old man for his birthday, and he'd been like a kid with a new toy ever since.

"Of course." She shook her head. "I don't know what he's going to do once winter sets in."

"Jude," said Carly, "could I get you to take these baked potatoes outside for me?" She gestured to the large cast-iron pot atop the stove.

"Sure thing." He freed himself from Lucas's grip, grabbed the pot and made his way through the mudroom and outside onto the deck that spanned one side of the house.

Strings of patio lights illuminated the area as Lily smoothed black-and-white-checkered tablecloths over the two wooden picnic tables. His nieces Kenzie, Matt's daughter, and Piper followed behind her, setting out mason jars full of sunflowers as centerpieces. Meanwhile, Noah ignited two patio heaters to ward off tonight's chill.

In front of the deck, his niece Megan, Andrew's daughter, and Lily's son, Colton, took turns adding wood to the metal firepit as orange flames reached toward the night sky.

"All right, you two." Andrew eyed the preteens over the railing. "That's enough wood for now."

Jude continued on to the far end of the deck where his father and brothers Andrew, Matt and Daniel stood near the grill, no doubt solving the world's problems while the steaks cooked.

"Potatoes are ready." He set the pot beside the grill as the sound of tires on gravel met his ears. That could only mean one thing. Turning, he saw Kayla's blue truck ease to a stop near the opposite end of the deck.

Lily hurried down the wooden steps to greet her with Noah in tow.

Jude watched as Lily introduced the two. Both smiled and shook hands before Noah wrapped an arm around his intended and pulled her close.

"Guess we'd best go say hello." Dad started across the expanse, followed by Matt and Daniel.

Andrew paused, looking at Jude. "Aren't you coming?"

"Why?" After their run-in earlier today, she probably wasn't that eager to see him either.

"Okay, but you're likely to have the old man barking at you if you don't."

Reluctantly, he dragged himself away from the warmth of the grill as the other women spilled from the house, giddy with excitement. He watched as everyone welcomed their guest, recalling the first time he'd brought Kayla home to meet his family. Was she as nervous now as she'd been that day?

Of course, back then, his mother had quickly put her at ease.

When she finally made her way onto the deck, Jude found it difficult to breathe. She was still the most beautiful woman he'd ever seen. Gone were this morning's braid and overalls, replaced by an ultrafeminine purple sweater, skinny jeans and riding boots. And her hair. He'd always liked it when she wore it down. Dark as chocolate and smooth as silk. Even now he could remember the exotic fragrance of her shampoo and wondered if she still smelled the same.

She stopped beside him, her lips tilting upward as her dark gaze captured his. "We meet again."

Unable to stop himself, he inhaled deep. But it was the aroma of an open fire and sizzling meat that brought him to his senses. "Guess we should get used to that."

"If you ladies want to bring out the rest of the food." Dad nodded at Hillary, Carly and Lacie. "The steaks are ready, so let's eat."

The meal had barely begun when talk of the wedding started, escalating Jude's desire to retreat. But for the sake of Noah and Lily, he hung around and enjoyed dessert. At least until Lily decided to walk Kayla through the layout of the event that would take place at the ranch next week.

After helping clear the tables, he made his escape, certain no one had seen him. Not that the entire family wouldn't know where to find him.

Once inside his shop, he flipped on the lights and breathed in the scent of wood. He needed to get ahold of himself. So what if Kayla was staying in Ouray? He was an easygoing guy. A cop, for crying out loud. He knew how to keep his cool. Yet twice in the last two days he'd lost it in front of her. She'd never gotten to him like that before. Why now?

Because Kayla had wounded his ego and

broken his heart. One day they were talking and texting, making plans to see one
another, and then nothing. She never com-
municated with him again. And though he
called and texted until he was blue in the
face, there was nothing until the record-
ing saying her number was no longer in
service.

Yet, like a fool, he'd continued to hold
out hope that he'd hear from her again.
The least she could have done was give
him an explanation instead of leaving him
to wonder.

Needing to redirect his thoughts, he
moved to the packaging area of the shop
to double-check an order. Then he heard
the door open.

He looked up, surprised to find Kayla
moving toward him.

His gaze narrowed as he rounded the
worktable. "Are you lost?"

"No, I was looking for you." Stopping in
front of him, she said, "I wanted to apologize for my behavior earlier today. You

were only thinking of the well-being of my baby."

Unexpected disappointment wove through him. As if she would have said that she'd made a mistake. That she'd once loved him, too, and wanted to try again. Stupid.

"No big deal. It's not like no one's ever gotten in my face before."

She scuffed her boot through a pile of sawdust. "I know. But you didn't deserve to be chastised, especially when you were only trying to help."

Not knowing what else to say, he simply nodded.

Kayla didn't say anything either, until… "Are you going to be okay with me staying in Ouray? Working together and stuff?"

Was she kidding? No, he wasn't okay. The last time they'd worked together, things had been different. They'd been a couple. Something he still found himself wishing for, no matter how much he didn't want to.

But he wasn't about to tell her that. "It's not like we haven't worked together before."

Hands clasped in front of her now, she looked almost shy. "I know. But that was before."

Yeah, before you cut me out of your life without even bothering to tell me.

After studying the space for a moment, Kayla moved toward a shelf stocked with finials and spindles. "You made these?"

"Yes."

She picked up a spindle, turning it this way and that before smoothing a hand over the surface. "They're beautiful. How'd you get started?"

Therapy, he wanted to say, having made numerous items immediately after she left and more when he didn't hear from her. But that would make him sound pathetic.

"Remember that house we worked on?" he said instead. "How some of the moldings and balusters outside had rotted?"

She smiled. "I do. You told the boss you could replicate it."

"And that's exactly what I did. The boss told some others, and the next thing I knew..." He motioned to the rest of the shop.

"That's amazing." Returning the spindle to its place, she faced him again. "I'm really proud of you."

"Thanks." Though his response may have been simple, the thoughts and emotions her praise stirred had him taking a step back.

"Well…" She rocked back on her heels. "I guess I should get back to Lily." She turned to leave, but he couldn't let her go. Not when there were things he desperately needed to know.

"I'm curious."

She turned toward him. "About what?"

"Why wouldn't you take my calls? Respond to my texts?"

She puffed out an incredulous laugh. "Um, I'm not sure what you're talking about. But in case you've forgotten, the last time we talked, you said you were done. That you were too tired to do *this*—" she made air quotes with her fingers "—anymore."

"I was referring to the conversation, not us." He'd been exhausted from working cattle all day. "I told you that in my text the next day."

Her expression went blank. "You... texted me?"

"Tried calling you, too." At least a dozen times. "But you never picked up."

Her shoulders drooped. She blew out a breath. "That would be because at some point between our conversation and the next morning, I lost my phone."

"How is that possible? It was almost midnight my time when we talked."

"I know. I was still asleep when my parents pulled out the next morning. The only thing I've been able to figure is that I must have dropped it somewhere between the firepit where I was talking to you and the door to the RV because when I woke up, I turned that motorhome upside down trying to find it and came up empty-handed." The pain in her dark eyes said she was telling the truth. "I was devastated. Not only had I lost my phone, I'd lost every contact I had in it." Her gaze drifted to his. "Including yours."

His brain struggled to keep up with what she was saying. "You could have called the house. Landline numbers can usually be found online."

Nodding, she bit the corner of her lip. "I thought about it. Then I reminded myself what you'd said…"

"Wow." He scuffed a hand over his face, the reality of her words tearing through him like a ninety-mile-per-hour fastball. Everything he'd believed was a lie.

Hands hanging on his hips, all he could do was stare. "All these years, you thought I dumped you?"

She simply shrugged. "Things happen for a reason. Within days of arriving in Denver, my dad was diagnosed with kidney cancer and it had already spread. My family needed me."

He cringed, knowing all too well the flood of emotions those words set off.

"So, I grabbed another pay-as-you-go phone, not realizing I could have my old number transferred, and spent the next ten months helping my mom care for him."

"Of course, you did. You and your father were very close."

She nodded again. "By the time he passed, I was done with traveling. I had a good job, so for the first time in my life, I decided to stay put."

"What about your mother?"

She grinned. "She's still wandering the country in our old RV."

"That thing's still running?"

"I don't think it'll ever die."

They shared a laugh then. Just like old times.

When she peered up at him, there was a sincerity in her dark eyes, along with something else. Regret, maybe. Or was that just wishful thinking?

She poked a thumb over her shoulder. "I should get back to Lily."

"Of course." He walked her to the door and pulled it open, his heart twisted in knots. "Kayla?"

Her gaze met his.

"I'm sorry. For what I said, for the misunderstanding… I wouldn't have hurt you for anything."

"Funny, I know that now. I just wish I believed it back then."

Chapter Five

Kayla never expected this pregnancy thing would be so exhausting. Then again, these last couple of days had been a flurry of activity. Throw in Jude's revelation last night, that he hadn't broken up with her, and, well, she'd tossed and turned until at least 3:00 a.m. And while she'd made it to church this morning, she had to pass on Lily's lunch invitation, opting for a much-needed nap instead.

Buried under the covers of her bed at Granger House Inn, she rolled over to look at the clock on the antique side table.

3:30 p.m.?

She hadn't intended to sleep that long.

Not when she still needed to come up with a wedding gift for Lily.

Throwing off the comforter, she sat on the edge of the bed with a sudden craving for one of those froufrou coffee drinks. Something with chocolate and lots of whipped cream but without all the caffeine.

She stretched and yawned, then laid a hand against her belly. "How about we go get some fresh air?" Maybe a little exercise would help clear her brain, and if that coffee shop on Main Street happened to be open, even better.

Thirty minutes later, she exited Mouse's Coffee and Chocolates with a steaming cup of white hot chocolate in one hand and a Scraps cookie in the other. According to the sign, the cookie was a family recipe, however the "scraps" in the cookies varied depending on what chocolates they'd made recently. She took a bite, the blend of flavors delighting her taste buds.

Under a mixture of clouds and sun, she strolled up the sidewalk, the brisk autumn air cutting through her brain fog. She still couldn't believe she was going to be living in Ouray, surrounded by its untouched beauty and historic charm. It was a dream come true.

Well, almost.

Crossing the street, she continued up Fifth Avenue, recalling the night of her last phone call with Jude. It had been a little over a year since she'd left Ouray, yet they'd still talked almost every day, increasing their desire to see each other again. That night, while her parents slept inside their RV, she'd sat beside what was left of their campfire and told Jude they were returning to Colorado. The rest of the conversation was spent with him trying to talk her into coming back to Ouray, while she pushed for him to meet her in Denver. After all, he'd been in Ouray his whole life. She'd thought it would be fun for them to experience something new together.

Perhaps she'd pushed too hard.

"Kayla, you know I can't do that. I have commitments here."

"Can't or won't?"

His sigh had crackled through the line. "I'm too tired to do this anymore, Kayla. I'm done."

When the line had gone dead, she'd hugged the blanket tighter. And cried. Something she'd never done before. But then, she'd never been in love before either. And she'd blown it.

All these years, she'd believed that *I'm done* meant he'd broken up with her. Now she found out it was only the conversation he'd been ending?

No wonder Jude had looked at her so strangely that first day in the park. While she'd believed one thing, he'd spent all these years thinking she'd dumped him.

She paused at the corner, staring at the cloud-dotted sky. Why did she have to lose her phone? If she hadn't, things could have turned out so differently. Her life could have been different. She and Jude could be married and raising a family here in Ouray.

But things were different. *She* was different. Among a gazillion other things, she had a child to consider. And for his or her sake, she prayed that her decision to stay in Ouray was the right one. That this was where God wanted her. Because she was all too familiar with the consequences of bad choices.

Taking a sip of her hot chocolate, she continued around the corner. No point dwelling on the past. Like the Bible said, to everything there is a season, and a time to every purpose under heaven. If there was one thing she knew for certain, it was that God was in control. And it was time to start thinking about that wedding gift.

It needed to be something personal and unique. Lily was a wealthy woman, after all; she could buy anything she wanted. Kayla wanted to give her something from the heart. Something Noah and Lily could cherish for more than just a day. But what?

Winding onto another of Ouray's gravel side streets, she polished off her cookie and took in the gray volcanic rock of the amphitheater that hugged the town's eastern border. When her gaze lowered, she came to an abrupt stop.

She hadn't meant to come here. Yet, there it was. The house she'd renovated in her mind at least a thousand times. The one she'd fallen in love with seven years ago.

The cute little Victorian looked worse than she remembered, though. As if the whole house was frowning, with its drooping front porch and dilapidated shutters. And who had the brilliant idea to paint it that mustard yellow with raspberry trim? Like that would help. Oh, how she'd love to restore this house and make it smile again.

While she and Jude had spent much of their time together evaluating nearly every home in town, this was the only one they'd actually gone into. She could still remember the beautiful wainscoting and unique moldings hidden beneath layers of paint. And the bedroom with a wall of windows they'd agreed would make a perfect kid's room.

She straightened. Other than the wedding and the hotel, Jude was no longer a part of her life. Nor would he ever be. Still, the opportunity to renovate this house was one she'd jump on in a heartbeat. That is, if it was for sale.

Looking to see if there might be a sign, she admired the house next door. Another Victorian that someone had breathed new life into. She visually skimmed the gray-blue exterior with all of its intricate details before shifting her focus to the stunning flower garden in the side yard. And there in its midst was an arbor similar to the one Lily had pointed out at the bridal shop yesterday.

She studied it curiously. She'd heard it said that when God spoke He often repeated Himself so a person was sure to hear Him.

God, I know an arbor would be perfect. But where would I build it?

The sound of gravel crunching drew her attention to the street, where a police SUV moved slowly toward her. And inside was none other than Jude Stephens.

He eased to a stop in front of her and

rolled his window down. "Looks pretty bad, doesn't it?" He pointed to the yellow house.

Heat crept into her cheeks. "Yeah." He knew how much she'd loved this house.

"What are you up to?" Arm draped over the steering wheel, he continued to watch her.

"Just catching up with the town." She glanced at the arbor again, remembering not so much her conversation with Jude last night, but where it took place. His shop would be the perfect place to build an arbor. But first she'd have to ask him.

Drawing in a breath, she faced him again. "See that arbor over there?" She pointed.

"In that garden?"

"Yes."

"What about it?"

"When Lily and I were at the bridal shop yesterday, she showed me a wedding photo with an arbor similar to that. A couple had used it for an altar. She said she'd wanted to have something comparable but couldn't find one rustic enough." Kayla stepped closer to the vehicle. "Since I have yet to find the right wedding gift for her, I thought I could build her one. She could use it in the wedding and then later at their home."

"Where are you going to do that?"

"Well..." Standing beside the SUV, she dragged her boot through the gravel. "Could I build it in your shop?"

"I...don't know about that."

"Oh. Okay." He could have at least taken a moment to think about it. "I guess I'll just have to come up with something else." She returned to the sidewalk.

"On second thought." His words had her whirling back around. "I haven't gotten them a gift either." He drummed his fingers on the dash. "And something like that—" he pointed in the direction of the arbor "—would be more personal than something bought in a store." He seemed to ponder her request before meeting her gaze. "What if we built it together and made it from both of us?"

Together? That had never entered her thought process. But if that's what it took to give Lily the perfect gift...

"I'm willing to do that."

"Good." He checked his watch. "I get off work at five. What do you say we grab some dinner and talk about a design?"

Dinner? With Jude? "I can draw up something."

"Yes, but if it's going to be from both of us, I'd like to have some input, too. And it's not like we have a lot of time."

Suddenly her great idea didn't seem so great. The way he manipulated the situation... Sure Jude was a nice guy, but Shane had been nice, too. Charming even. It wasn't until after they were married that she'd seen his true colors.

Jude's not Shane. He wouldn't try to make you do anything you didn't want to do. But then, I think you already know that.

Lily's words replayed in her mind.

Contemplating the man before her, Kayla thought about the Jude she once knew. In many ways, he was the same man. But when it came to judging someone's character, she was a proven failure.

The guy only asked you to dinner—a public, working one at that. He's not looking for a lifetime commitment.

She really did want to do this arbor for Lily. And since it looked like this was her only option—

"All right. I'm craving stew. I'll meet you at O'Brien's at six. Don't be late."

Two days after an all-too-revealing discussion about his and Kayla's breakup, Jude was still trying to wrap his brain around the fact that it was nothing more than a misunderstanding that had torn the two of them apart. He still couldn't believe that she thought *he'd* broken things off. All the while, he'd been here, wondering why *she* refused to talk to him.

He shook his head. Trying to forget what you've believed for years wasn't easy. So, when Kayla had asked to use his shop, he'd been kind of taken aback. At least he'd managed to smooth over that mistake. By suggesting they work together, no less.

Still, over dinner last night, he'd realized just what a great idea the arbor was. Like Kayla, he didn't want to give his brother some cheesy, unmemorable gift that would be tucked away in a closet and forgotten. No, he'd much rather give Noah and Lily something with meaning and purpose. And an arbor would be just that.

Now, Jude and Kayla were on a mission. Armed with the collaborative design they'd come up with over dinner last night, it was time to get the lumber and hardware. Since it was already Monday and they intended to present Lily and Noah with the arbor at the rehearsal dinner Friday night, there wasn't much time.

Darkness surrounded them as they headed north on Highway 550 just before seven Monday evening. Typically, he made his trips to the home improvement store in the mornings, but with him on duty today and Kayla helping Lily with wedding preparations, there wasn't much choice.

Glancing toward the other side of the cab, he was reminded of all the times he and Kayla had made this same drive, usually for dinner or a movie. Except back then she would sit next to him and they'd talk the whole way. Now she hugged the other side of the vehicle, not saying a word. As though they were complete strangers.

He didn't like that at all.

Desperate to break the silence, he said, "Do you have your list?"

"Yes, but I'm wondering if we shouldn't make the arbor arched instead of squared."

"Why?" Last night she'd seemed to know exactly what she wanted.

"Because I want it be perfect."

"I thought it was supposed to be rustic? That negates perfection." Out of the corner of his eye, he saw her frown. "Okay, you said Lily showed you a photo. What did that arbor look like?"

"It was made of cedar."

"Arched or squared?"

"Squared."

He looked her way. "What's the problem then?" Why was she vacillating?

Her shoulder lifted. "I guess you're right."

Oh, he knew he was right. Question was, why didn't she? "Listen, Kayla, there isn't a right or wrong here. Lily will love it no matter what."

The corners of her mouth turned up ever so slightly. "Yeah, I think she will, too."

She thinks? That wasn't the Kayla he knew.

Tightening his grip on the steering wheel, he decided to change the subject. "What did you do today?"

"Lily and I worked on favors for the wedding guests, and I called my boss back in Denver."

Ah, turning in her resignation. "How did that go?"

"Better than I thought." She twisted to face him. "Evidently the guy who's covering for me is more than happy to stay on at the position permanently. My boss praised my work ethic, said the two weeks wasn't necessary, but he was still going to pay me for them."

"That's fantastic. He obviously thinks very highly of you and your work."

"He worries about me. You know, the whole widowed and pregnant thing."

"Don't discount yourself. You're a skilled worker. Though, let's face it, not every woman could handle the circumstances you've found yourself in."

"Yeah, well, sometimes things work out for the better."

He shot a curious glance her way as they approached Montrose, the city lights illuminating the cab. Why would she say such a thing? Wouldn't she prefer to share something as momentous as having a child with her husband? To have his help and support? Or was it a defense mechanism? Trying to make the most of a difficult situation?

"Oh, and I heard from my mother today."

Thoughts of Claudette Brennan made him smile. The woman was as nice as she could be, though a little on the eccentric side. As evidenced by the fact that she was now traveling the country alone. In an RV, no less. "Where is Claudette these days?"

"Florida. She's been working at a marina somewhere in the panhandle. And, apparently, she has a boyfriend."

"No kidding?" Pausing at a stoplight, he eyed Kayla. "How do you feel about that?"

"It's fine." She waved a hand. "It's not like he's the first. Though this one might be serious."

"Why do you say that?" He hit the gas pedal again.

"Because she spent thirty minutes telling me about his boat and how he wants to sail around the world."

"Sounds like she's found someone else with wanderlust. I can see it now. She trades traveling the US in an RV for traveling the world on a sailboat."

"I wouldn't put it past her."

He was glad to see they were finally enjoying a normal conversation. Too bad they were pulling up to the home improvement store.

He located a parking space and eased to a stop before turning off the engine. Exiting, he continued around the vehicle to assist Kayla, but she was already on her way to the entrance when he got there.

Frustrated, he grabbed an industrial panel cart on their way inside and headed straight for the lumber.

When they reached the cedar, he examined a couple of posts. "What do you think?" He held one vertically for a better view.

Kayla looked from the wood to him. "These are our only options?"

"In cedar, yes." Did she think they were going to have some exotic wood or something?

Crossing her arms over her chest, she cocked her head, sending her long hair spilling over her shoulder as she pursed her lips. "What are your thoughts?"

Seriously? "It's exactly what I had in mind."

She nodded then. "Okay."

Okay? "Is this or is this not what you envisioned?"

"Yeah. It's fine."

He loaded what they needed onto the cart, wondering where all this second-guessing had come from. "All right. Is that everything?"

She looked at her list, then counted the wood pieces. "Yes. We just need some screws and brackets."

"All right, lead the way."

They continued on to the hardware section.

Kayla picked out two different brackets. "Which one do you like?" She held them up. One more ornate while the other was plain and simple.

"That one." He pointed to the second one.

"Oh." Looking disappointed, she stared at them a moment. "If you say so." She started to put the ornate one back.

"Wait a minute." He reached a hand to stop her. "This is supposed to be a joint project." Good grief, how was she ever going to make any headway at the hotel when she questioned everything? "Which one do you like?"

Again, she studied them. "The simple one." Grabbing what she needed, she started to set them on the cart.

But he stopped her. Something wasn't right. "Kayla, is something wrong? You seem to be second-guessing yourself on everything tonight. Do you not want to do this anymore?"

Her chestnut eyes wide, she looked up at him. "Of course, I do. This gift is important to me."

"Then what's the problem?"

She considered him for a long moment before shaking her head. "I'm sorry. I guess I'm just tired." Her hand went to her belly. "This pregnancy thing seems to wear me out a lot faster than usual." She drew in a breath. "The cedar is perfect, and we'll go with…" She contemplated the bracket choices. "*This* hardware." Tossing the simple version he'd chosen initially onto the cart, she added, "After all, it's supposed to be rustic."

Again, she glanced at her list before sending a smile his way. Forced as it may be. "My list is complete."

"All right, let's get out of here then." And hopefully, she'd be well rested tomorrow when they started the project.

Chapter Six

When Kayla woke up the next morning, she was struck by two things: she was without a job, and she and Jude had only three nights left to get the arbor built and decorated before presenting it to Lily and Noah. And she wanted it to be perfect.

Okay, she wasn't really without a job. She just wouldn't begin work on the hotel until after the wedding was out of the way. Acquiring permits would take top priority, then hiring a crew. Research would be involved in both, though when it came to hiring, she was definitely at a disadvantage.

Back in Denver, she had contacts. Even in a big city, word of mouth was a powerful resource. She didn't know anyone in Ouray, except Lily, Jude and his family. Then again, his brother Andrew was a builder. Perhaps he'd have some suggestions. She'd need a couple of good carpenters as well as some men or women who could do just about anything from demo to grunt work to painting. And of course, they'd need to have experience working with historical buildings. Something that shouldn't be too difficult in Ouray, given the large percentage of Victorian-era structures.

She'd think about that next week, though. Tonight, she had an arbor to build. Fortunately for her, Lily and Noah had some event at the school, so she wouldn't have to worry about them seeing her arrive. Not only would she hate to spoil the surprise, there was no telling what they might think if they caught her and Jude holed up in his shop. However, an arbor would probably be the furthest thing from their minds, so she supposed that was okay. This time.

The sun was setting when she bumped

up the drive of Abundant Blessings Ranch. She parked on the far side of Jude's black pickup, hoping it might hide her blue truck, then drew in a deep breath before getting out. She needed to keep it together tonight. Jude was not Shane. Yet when he got frustrated because of her indecision…

Her eyes closed briefly, and she took another breath. *Help me, Lord.*

She grabbed her tool belt from the crossover toolbox in the bed of her truck before hurrying into Jude's shop.

He was standing in the middle of the space and jerked his head in her direction as she entered. "'Bout time you got here."

Her steps slowed. Hadn't they agreed on six o'clock? She wasn't late.

Hands low on his denim-covered hips, he stepped around one of the cedar posts. "You might want to lock that door."

She gave the deadbolt a twist, wondering why he felt the need to start barking out orders. He was reminding her of someone else.

Jude isn't Shane.

Turning, she approached the space where he had all of the wood laid out. "Looks good. Much better than it did at the store."

"Yeah, well, the store didn't exactly have the best lighting."

She eyed the bright bulbs stretching the length of Jude's shop. "That's certainly not a problem here."

His gaze followed hers. "I do a lot of detail work and that requires good lighting, so I don't skimp."

"I want to thank you again for allowing me to use your shop."

"Me?" His dark brow lifted. "I thought it was *we*?"

"That's what I meant." Her shoulder automatically lifted. "I just—"

"It's all right, Kayla." He sent her a look that was somewhere between annoyed and amused. "I was just yankin' your chain."

"Of course you were." She fastened her tool belt around her hips, something that was more challenging than the last time she'd worn it.

"You look cute like that." Jude's sudden

shift from annoyed to charming reminded her of her late husband, ratcheting her anxiety.

"Let's get this thing built." So she could get away without making a fool of herself.

A short time later, Jude turned off the miter saw and moved his goggles to the top of his head. "Hey, I have an idea. Since we want to make this personal, what if I carve a phrase or something?"

"Won't that take a long time?"

"Not necessarily. Though it would be easier to do it before it's assembled, which means we probably wouldn't be able to finish tonight."

"But we need to get it done."

"We'll still have two more nights."

The fact that he was right bugged her. Then again, she didn't exactly want to spend any more time here than necessary.

"No, because I don't know what Lily might have planned and my whole point of being here this week was to help her."

"Point taken."

Over the next two hours, they assembled

the sides and top of the arbor. Even though they'd done it before, Kayla was surprised by how well they worked together. Now all they needed to do was to join the top portion to the sides.

"Where are those brackets we bought?"

"In that bag over there." He pointed to one of the worktables.

She crossed the room, grabbed the bag and pulled out the brackets, her heart stopping. There were only three. "Did you take one out?"

He looked at her matter-of-factly. "No."

"There are only three in this bag. Could it have fallen out in your truck?"

"You can check."

"I'll be right back." She hurried outside, sweat beading her brow despite the cool night air. Opening the back door of the cab, she hunted high and low before moving on to the front seat. Her breath quickened. It wasn't here.

She slammed the door and returned to the shop, where she checked every surface.

"You didn't find it?"

"No." Panic flitted through her. Without that last bracket, they couldn't finish the arbor.

Jude picked up the bag and reached inside. "According to the receipt, we only bought three brackets."

"What?" She moved beside him, grabbed the strip of paper and stared at it. "How could I be so stupid?" She growled. "I can't believe I did that."

"Why are you being so hard on yourself?" Brow puckered, he looked at her as if she was crazy. "It's not that big a deal. You can just pick up another one tomorrow."

"But we won't be able to finish it tonight. We're giving it to them in *three days*."

"Which means we still have time to pick up the bracket. *And* I'll have time to do the carving."

Turning, she rubbed her arms. "I shouldn't have forgotten it."

He stepped in front of her. Arms crossed, he looked down at her, making her wince.

"You know, you used to be so confident.

What happened? Last night you kept second-guessing yourself, and now you're blowing this one little thing totally out of proportion. Why?"

Because the last two years of her life were spent with someone who didn't hesitate to point out her shortcomings.

She dared a look into Jude's dark eyes. Yet instead of censure, all she saw was confusion and compassion. Along with an honest desire to know what had changed. But she couldn't give him that.

"You're right." She took a deep breath. "Once again, I'm stressing about the wedding. Or at least, getting this done in time."

"Well, stop it. Stress isn't good for you or the baby." He started to turn, then grinned her way. "Yeah, I just told you what to do. Deal with it."

A smile tugged at the corners of her mouth. As dangerous as it might be, she kind of appreciated his concern. Not that she was about to tell him that.

"I'll try to overlook it."

"That's good, because we've got work

to do." He pulled out his phone. "That reminds me, what's your number?"

Why did he want her number? Her curiosity didn't stop her from rattling it off, though.

Next thing she knew, her own phone was vibrating. She pulled it from her back pocket and looked at the screen.

"That's just me." He tucked his device into his pocket. "Now you have my number. In case you think of anything else concerning the arbor."

"Good idea." Not that she had any plans to call him. About the arbor or anything else.

Between work and helping Kayla with the arbor, Jude was getting behind on his orders. So, as he waited for her to arrive Thursday evening, he was determined to get as many packaged and ready to go out tomorrow as he possibly could.

After taping and labeling one box, he grabbed another, along with an order, and moved to his turned baluster inventory.

Since Carly had planned a girls' night out for Lily, Lacie and Kayla last night, it gave him the opportunity to knock out the carving on the arbor, add the extra bracket Kayla had dropped off to finish the assembly and then tackle some other wood projects he had hanging over his head. He did his best to have a two-to five-day turnaround on all internet orders. But considering that most of what he sold online was stock items, he often got them out even faster.

Builder orders, though, were usually on a much larger scale and involved a specific delivery date. And the one he was currently working on for a contractor in Telluride was his largest yet. Fortunately, the delivery date was still a few weeks out, and he was ahead of schedule. Still, this week had really slowed him down.

He closed the now-filled box, glancing at the tarp-covered arbor tucked discreetly into one corner of the shop. He couldn't wait to see Kayla's reaction. When he'd awoken yesterday morning, an idea for the inscription had been impressed on his heart so deeply it couldn't be ignored. Of course, he wasn't about to proceed without Kayla's approval, so he'd texted her his thoughts and gotten the okay.

Working with her on this project had been an eye-opening experience. Initially, he'd viewed her as the same girl he'd known seven years ago. But after spending time with her, he'd seen how much she'd changed—and not necessarily for the better.

How did Kayla go from being confident and carefree to uncertain and troubled? Had her husband's death left her feeling insecure? She was pregnant and alone, after all. That would be a scary scenario for anyone.

Whatever the case, he longed to help her regain her confidence. How he would do that, though, he didn't have a clue. But he supposed he could start by simply being her friend.

After printing another label, he affixed it to the box as the door opened. He looked up, expecting to see Kayla, but it was his father ambling toward him.

"You busy?"

"Just packaging some orders." Jude tapped the box, purposely keeping the fact that he was waiting on Kayla to himself. Dad would only want to know why she was coming, and Jude had promised to keep the arbor a secret.

The old man stood at the opposite side of the table, his beige felt cowboy hat tipped back to reveal his thick salt-and-pepper hair. "You've been spending a lot of time in here."

Jude added the box to his stack on the floor. "Can't let my customers down."

"How many customers are we talking about?" Dad looked curious.

Jude wasn't about to pass up the opportunity to impress upon his father that his woodworking wasn't just a hobby. That it was a successful business, leaving Jude little time to worry about cattle. "A dozen just this week. And a builder out of Telluride wants some corbels and moldings, along with window and door casings." He motioned toward the work-in-progress behind him.

His father eyed the stack of cove moldings next to Jude's table saw. "Must be a big house."

"Several houses, actually." Moving to the pile, Jude motioned for his old man to follow. "And he's looking to do even more." He picked up a length. "I'm kind of stoked about this particular design. It's a little out of the ordinary, but it really shows off the beauty of this walnut." He smoothed his hand across the surface.

Dad did the same. "You do some mighty fine work, all right."

"Thank you." Maybe the old man was finally getting it.

Shoving his hands into the pockets of his worn Wranglers, his father moved away. "We're going to need to work cattle soon. Winter could arrive anytime, and I want to make sure we're ready. How does next week look for you?"

Disappointment flooded Jude's veins. "I don't know. I'm kind of behind."

His father looked at him, his gaze narrowing. "Have you thought any more about our discussion last week?"

Jude's jaw muscles clenched. He'd thought about it, all right. Mostly about how to tell the old man he wanted no part of cattle ranching. He longed for his father's approval. But was it worth it if it meant giving up his dream?

"Between work, the wedding and helping Noah with the rodeo school, I've been pretty busy." Since the school's grand opening in September, they'd all pitched in to help ensure its success.

"Yeah, I reckon this past month has been a little topsy-turvy for all of us."

Cool air filtered into the metal building just then, and he and his dad both turned to find Kayla closing the door behind her.

"Hello, Clint." She continued toward them, looking prettier than someone in work clothes had a right to.

"Kayla." Dad grinned, tipping his hat. "What are you two working on tonight?"

And there it was. That gleam in Dad's eye. The one Jude had seen for the past couple of months as the old man played matchmaker for Noah and Lily. And though he may have been successful with them, Jude and Kayla were a different story. So his father might as well take his crazy notions and move on down the road.

Without missing a beat, Kayla said, "Oh, we're simply comparing notes for Saturday. Making sure we're on the same page as far as keeping the bride and groom from seeing each other before the ceremony."

"That's right." Dad chuckled. "With both of them living here at the ranch, that could be challenging."

"Yes, especially when I know Lily is going to want to be here when the crew is setting up and decorating that tent."

"Well, let me know if you need any help keeping ol' Noah out of the way. I ought to be able to come up with something."

Jude eyed the man. "If we could just keep him confined to the stables, that'd help."

With a smile, the old man nodded. "I'll see what I can do." His dark gaze shifted from Kayla to Jude and back. "In the meantime, I'd best leave you two alone to conspire." He started for the door.

Kayla watched him leave. "Good to see you again, Clint."

"Likewise, young lady." He halted his retreat. "I hear you're going to be staying in Ouray."

She glanced at Jude before responding. "That is correct."

"Well, don't you be a stranger then. You're welcome at the ranch anytime."

Hoping to hurry the man along, Jude said, "Good night, Dad."

"Night, son." He waved on his way out the door.

When the door finally closed, Jude and Kayla busted out laughing.

"He hasn't changed a bit, has he?" said Kayla.

"A little more cantankerous, maybe,

but other than that..." He smiled at the woman who stood a good seven or eight inches shorter than his six-feet-two-inches. "Thank you, by the way."

"For what?"

"Saving me."

"What did I save you from?"

"My father." Turning, he eased toward the door and locked it.

"Oh?" The lilt of her voice said she was curious.

He moved toward the corner, pausing beside the arbor. "You'll be happy to know that the arbor is complete, including the carving. All you have to do is add the lights and anything else you want."

For a moment, her gaze narrowed on him, as though she was annoyed with the change in subject.

So, he waited until she said, "Are you going to let me see it or not?"

He carefully tugged off the tarp, surprised by the anxiety that had suddenly taken hold of him. What if she didn't like it?

Tossing the tarp aside, he sucked in a breath and waited.

Tears filled her eyes as she read the engraved words. Unfortunately, he was too ignorant to know if they were sad or happy tears. He could only pray—

"It's beautiful, Jude."

Air audibly whooshed from his lungs. "You mean, you like the inscription?"

"Yes. It's absolutely perfect." Standing on tiptoes, she fingered the words. "'And the two shall become one.'"

"I thought it was appropriate. Both for the wedding and as an ongoing reminder as they begin their new life together."

"I'm just annoyed that I didn't think of that myself."

Standing back, he admired the final product. "Your design, my carving. I think we're looking at the epitome of teamwork."

"We always did work well together."

"Yeah, we did." Until it came to their most important collaboration of all. In his mind, she'd given up and walked away, leaving him with a broken heart and broken dreams. And though he knew differently now, that was still one unfinished project he didn't want to delve into ever again.

Chapter Seven

Kayla was going to be late. A matron of honor was not supposed to be late for her best friend's rehearsal dinner.

Nonetheless, she stood there staring into her closet at the bed-and-breakfast. Seemed her miniscule selection of "nice" clothes was dwindling by the day.

That's because you keep getting bigger.

Her hand automatically went to her belly. "Sweet thing, you sure are putting a crimp in my style." Not that she had any style. No, that was Lily's forte. Still, she wasn't about to wear overalls to her best friend's wedding rehearsal. There had to be something.

Shoving the hangers left and right, she grabbed the only pair of skinny jeans that still fit. At least they had last Saturday. Today was anybody's guess. She huffed out a breath. Whether she liked it or not, it was time to buy some real maternity clothes.

After deciding on a turquoise bohemian-style tunic, she set to work again, tossing her previous selection into a pile with outfits one and two before donning her fourth, and final, choice.

She could hardly wait to see Lily's face when they presented the arbor to her and Noah. Though she really should have thought things through a little better before she agreed to let Jude help her.

Where would you have built it then? Carly's backyard?

Okay, so having his help was logical. Still, she hadn't considered just how much time it would involve spending with him. Or the fond memories their collaboration would stir. Throw in her indecision and virtual meltdown...

She supposed it was worth it, though. The whole thing had turned out better than she'd imagined, thanks in large part to Jude's inscription. Because of that one thing, their gift was every bit as unique and personal as Kayla had hoped.

Besides, the wedding was almost over. After that, there would be no need for her to see Jude. Sure, they'd probably run into each other now and then in town, but it would be months before he'd be needed at the hotel.

A knock sounded at the door as she checked her reflection in the cheval mirror.

"Kayla, it's Carly."

She hurried to the door and swung it open. "Hey."

"We're heading out to the ranch now and wanted to see if you needed a ride."

"Aw, thank you. But I'm staying with Lily tonight."

"Oh, that's right." Carly waved a hand, her gray-blue eyes traversing Kayla's attire. "Cute outfit, by the way."

Kayla looked down, a hint of relief washing over her. "You think so?"

"I wouldn't have said it if I didn't."

She let go a sigh. "Good, because it's the only thing that fits."

The cute blonde chuckled. "Don't I know it." She paused for a moment, her brow puckering. "Wait. I've got all kinds of maternity clothes I don't need anymore. I'd be happy to give them to you."

"That's funny because I was just telling myself it was time to go shopping for some."

"Nonsense. I'll haul them out this weekend, and you can go through them at your leisure."

"Oh, that would be wonderful." She stepped forward to give her hostess a hug. "Thank you."

Somewhere outside a horn honked, and Carly jumped. "Oops, they're waiting on me." She started down the stairs.

"I'll be right behind you," Kayla hollered after her.

Back in her room, she quickly put on her

boots and ran a brush through her hair before tossing it into her overnight bag. After one final check to make sure she had everything, she was out the door.

A few moments later, she tossed her bag into the cab of her truck and hopped inside. Jamming the key in the ignition, she gave it a turn. But instead of turning over, the engine groaned in protest.

She tried again, only to get the same results. Except the groan was more like a pathetic whine.

"Oh, no, no, no, no, no."

Again, she tried, willing the thing to start. But it refused.

She popped the hood and hopped out. The sun had already dipped below the town's western slope, leaving only shadows in its wake, so she had to use the flashlight on her phone. She checked the connections on the battery and tried one more time.

Still nothing.

Now she was really going to be late.

She dialed Lily, but the call went straight to voice mail.

Looking up and down the street, she contemplated asking somebody to give her a jump. But who? There was no one around, and she didn't relish the idea of knocking on a stranger's door. Too bad Carly didn't have any other guests.

She tried Lily again. Nothing.

Peering down at the numbers on her screen, she couldn't help noticing the missed call from Jude Tuesday night. He was the last person she wanted to call. Aside from all of the other reasons, he'd already come to her rescue twice. First with her tire and then again at the hotel when she screamed.

No, she definitely did not want to call him.

This is a rehearsal dinner, you know. As in, you're supposed to be there.

She whimpered. "Why, God?"

Reluctantly, she tapped a finger to Jude's name and set the phone to her ear. Maybe he wouldn't answer.

"Kayla?"

Her shoulders slumped. "I have a problem."

"No kidding. You're supposed to be here."

"I'm aware of that, but my truck won't start and Andrew and Carly already left."

"They're pulling up the drive as we speak."

Was he trying to make her feel worse?

She heard noises on his end of the line. Shuffling noises, then a thud. "Could you please send someone to give me a jump?"

"No, because I'm already on my way."

"You're—"

"And at this point, there's no time for a jump, so I'll just have to bring you out here. We'll worry about your truck later."

Well, that was just peachy.

She waited on the front porch of Granger House Inn until she saw Jude's truck round the corner. He'd barely come to a stop before she opened the door and threw herself and her overnight bag inside.

Across the cab, he smirked. "You look like you're in a hurry."

She glowered, more frustrated with herself than anything. "Just drive."

When they arrived at the ranch fifteen minutes later, Lily was waiting for her.

"I'm so sorry," Kayla said, approaching her friend.

"It's not your fault." Lily smiled, looking much calmer than Kayla and far more put together. "So, take a deep breath and shake it off before we get started with the rehearsal."

Kayla did as she was told, taking the opportunity to roll her head from side to side, too, in hopes of working out the kinks. She blew out a long breath. "Okay, I'm good."

"Excellent." Lily slipped her arm through Kayla's as they started toward the open area behind the house where a massive tent would be constructed tomorrow to host the big event. "Besides, God has a reason for everything."

Kayla knew her friend was right, however the fact that Lily's gaze suddenly moved from her to Jude wasn't helping.

"Before we get started with the rehearsal—" Jude stepped in front of them, halting their progress "—we need to create the proper atmosphere." He winked at her then. "Don't you agree, Kayla?"

She ignored the unwanted heat creeping into her cheeks and broke free of Lily. "Yes, absolutely. Setting is always important, even in rehearsals."

Noah came alongside Lily. "Just what are you up to, Jude?"

"Kayla, why don't you keep an eye on these two?" He pointed between the bride and groom before turning his attention to his other brothers. "Daniel, Matt and Andrew, come with me."

The brothers followed him without question, continuing into his shop.

Excitement bubbled inside of Kayla. "Where are you planning to do the actual run-through?"

Lily looked at her suspiciously. "Right over there." She pointed to the large clearing where some portable floodlights illuminated the bench seating that was already occupied by Clint, Hillary, Carly, Lacie and the kids.

Kayla grinned at the happy couple and motioned in that direction. "Shall we then?" Glancing behind her, she saw the men were already out the door with the arbor and heading in the same direction.

They reached the benches as the brothers bypassed them and settled the tarp-covered arbor on the ground. Jude had told her during their ride out here that he'd temporarily attached boards to the bottoms of the arbor's posts, running from front to back on each side to give it more stability on the grass. Once it was moved to its permanent home, it would be set into the ground with concrete.

"Thanks, guys." Grinning, Jude rubbed his hands together in anticipation as he moved beside Kayla. "Ready?"

She nodded, then turned to address Lily and Noah. "Jude and I didn't know what to get you guys for a wedding present. So, since you two are kind of hard to buy for, we decided to make you something."

"Something you could use for the wedding and for many years to come," added Jude.

Lily watched them, her green eyes wide with delight as she practically bubbled with anticipation.

Kayla peered up at Jude. "I think we should go ahead and give it to them before Lily explodes."

Laughter filled the cool evening air as she and Jude moved to either side of the arbor. They took hold of the tarp.

"Everybody ready?" asked Jude.

"One," they all shouted in unison. "Two. Three."

With that, Jude and Kayla unveiled their surprise.

Lily gasped, her hand promptly covering her mouth. Tears filled her eyes as she read the inscription. "Oh, you guys." She moved in to hug Kayla and Jude. "This is so beautiful."

"Like the one you showed me at the bridal shop," Kayla said.

Her friend shook her head. "It's better. Because you made it. And that carving… That makes it even more special."

"That was Jude's idea."

"It couldn't be more perfect," said Lily.

"You two are quite the team," added Noah, throwing in a couple hugs of his own.

Kayla glanced at Jude. Despite everything, they had, indeed, come together to create something Noah and Lily would cherish both now and in the future.

But being a team involved more than a common goal. Trust had to be built. One had to know that the other would be there when they needed them, that they had their back and wouldn't tear them down in order to make themselves feel better.

As everyone moved in to inspect their handiwork, Jude put his mouth near Kayla's ear.

"You done good."

Shivers skittered down her spine as she gazed into his eyes. "Right back atcha."

Noah's wedding day had finally arrived, and Jude would be glad when it was over.

His big brother would be the third member of the Stephens family to get married in the last thirteen months. Throw in Matt and Lacie's announcement last night that they were expecting a baby in May, and all this wedded bliss was getting to be too much for Jude.

Waiting for the morning's second pot of coffee to brew, he found himself bombarded by thoughts of Kayla. He'd witnessed a side of her this week that had him shuffling through old memories, trying to recall if he'd ever seen that kind of insecurity in her before. He continued to come up empty-handed, though, which only served to drive him nuts, wondering what had happened in the past seven years.

And then last night came along, bringing with it a glimpse of the old Kayla. The one who knew what she wanted and refused to let anything stand in her way. The one who confidently stood before his entire family to present Noah and Lily with a heartfelt gift. It had made him proud to be at her side. Did she have any idea how gorgeous she was? How her turquoise shirt highlighted her chestnut eyes? And the way her long, silky hair spilled down her back had him longing to run his fingers through it.

He snagged a mug from the cupboard beside the sink, then slammed the door with a little too much force. Why did she have to look so good? And why had her truck picked last night of all nights to break down? He'd have been fine if she'd just shown up. Instead her slightly sweet, slightly floral fragrance wrapped around him as they drove, reminding him of another time when she would have been his date. Even when he and Noah returned later to Granger House to start her vehicle, her aroma lingered in the cab of Jude's truck, teasing and tormenting him all the way back to the ranch, and then even as he slept.

He filled his cup and grabbed a cinnamon roll from the foil pan on the stove. That was one of the benefits of Dad's relationship with Hillary Ward-Thompson. Her daughter, Celeste Purcell, owned Granny's Kitchen, a diner in town where they made some of the finest cinnamon rolls in the country. Light and fluffy, oozing with cinnamony goodness…

Seemed Hillary was always eager to drop a pan or two by the house. Either that or Dad was going into town to pick some up.

Dawn illuminated the horizon as Jude stepped outside onto the deck. Steam billowed from his mug. The air was crisp and the sky clear. A welcome sight after the unexpected storm that had blown through overnight. But this morning held the promise of a beautiful autumn day.

Across the drive, he saw Dad and Hillary exit the barn, talking and laughing. As always, Hillary was stylishly dressed, save for the black rubber boots his father had given her this past spring. Now she could join him as he moved around the ranch without having to worry about messing up her fancy footwear.

Beside her, Dad wore his usual denim work shirt along with Wranglers, work boots and his well-worn beige felt Stetson. The couple presented quite a contrast, that's for sure. And even though Hillary was the antithesis of Jude's mother, this seemingly mismatched couple made a good pairing, like bacon and maple syrup.

Jude watched as the old man reached for Hillary's hand and held it as they walked toward him, oblivious to his presence. So much for Dad's claim that they were only friends. Not that Jude and his brothers hadn't already figured it out. They just weren't sure if their father was trying to convince them or himself.

Hillary was the first to spot him as they started up the steps of the deck. "Good morning, Jude."

Dad promptly let go of her hand. "Son. I didn't see you there." He looked as nervous as a teenage boy who just got busted by his girlfriend's father.

And Jude couldn't pass up the opportunity to mess with him. "Obviously." He grinned.

The old man cleared his throat. "When are those people supposed to be here to set up the tent?"

"Seven thirty." Jude glanced at his watch. Seven ten. "So anytime." They'd be followed by decorators and caterers...

"This is going to be a busy place, that's for sure." Hillary didn't appear to be the least bit rattled. "Poor Lily's going to have a tough time staying away." She paused for a moment. "I have a pan of cinnamon rolls I need to run down to the cabin. Perhaps I'll ask her if there's anything she'd like me to do."

"Yeah, you're good at bossing people around."

Hillary's brow lifted, her laser focus honing in on his father. "One does not make it to the top of the corporate ladder without knowing how to take charge." Until a few years ago, she'd been a high-ranking executive at one of the world's largest oil companies.

"Oh, you certainly know how to do that, woman."

She simply grinned, no doubt proud of her reputation. "Jude, I meant to tell you, that arbor you and Kayla made for Noah and Lily was absolutely stunning."

His smile evaporated, his heart sinking. "Oh, no. I forgot about the arbor." He set his mug on the nearest horizontal surface and hurried down the steps. "The storm."

While Kayla had insisted they move it back inside his shop, he'd argued that it would be just fine next to the building. Now he could only pray he was right.

Determined steps propelled him up the gravel driveway and past his shop. A cow bellowed in the distance, something he was likely to do, too, if anything happened to that arbor.

He yanked up the sleeves of his gray Henley as he rounded the corner, then came to an abrupt stop.

A few feet away, the arbor lay on the

ground, misshapen, with one side collapsed. The storm had blown it over.

Why hadn't he listened to Kayla?

Because he'd been eager to take care
of her truck and hadn't anticipated bad
weather.

Staring down at the dilapidated mess,
he scratched a hand through his hair. This
was not good.

A low growl escaped him as he knelt for
a closer inspection. Some of the cedar had
split around the screws. Slats were crooked
and a couple were broken. Kayla was going
to be heartbroken. Not to mention angry.
He could only hope she'd place the blame
on him, where it was due, and not try to
shoulder it herself.

Better yet, he'd just fix it before she
found out.

He pushed to his feet and turned just in
time to see her moving toward him, a hor-
rified look on her face.

"What happened?"

"Storm blew it over."

Her eyes welled with tears, panic creased her pretty brow. "What are we going to do?"

"Fix it before the bride and groom find out. Where's Lily?"

"She's still back at the cabin. I'm supposed to call her when the coast is clear."

"What?"

"It's her wedding day. Noah isn't supposed to see her before the wedding. He needs to be out of the way when she comes to check on the setup crew."

"All right. Dad can handle that. It'll give him something to do." Again, he surveyed the arbor. "In the meantime, I need to have this fixed by the time they get that tent set up." It was supposed to serve as the altar, after all.

Movement had his gaze flitting toward the drive. "Great. Here comes the setup crew now."

Kayla continued to fret. "I should have insisted we put it back in the shop last night."

There she went, blaming herself again.

But he wasn't about to let her get away with it. Not today.

He took a step closer. "This is not your fault, Kayla, so don't even go there. You asked me to put it in the shop, but I said it would be fine. So, if you want to blame anyone, blame me."

Eyes wide, she simply blinked. Finally, she nodded.

"All right. I'm going to get someone to help me move this into the shop while you show the crew where to put up the tent."

Chapter Eight

The late-afternoon sun was warm as Kayla waited for the wedding to start, feeling more nervous than she'd been at her own wedding. Then again, her wedding had been a small affair, with only her mom and Shane's family in attendance. Shane had said he'd rather spend the money on the honeymoon than the wedding, so that's what they'd done. Little had she known he'd be spending most of that money on drinks. It was the first time she'd seen him inebriated. Though definitely not the last. She'd never forget him looking at her with glassy eyes, his speech slurred as he announced that she was no fun and he never should have married her.

Of course, in typical Shane fashion, he'd apologized profusely the next day, promising it would never happen again. If she had a dollar for every time she'd heard that, she'd be a wealthy woman.

Instead she'd allowed him to rob her of her dignity and self-confidence. Never again would she let someone wield that kind of power over her.

Straightening, she shook off the memory and drew in a deep breath laced with the fragrance of off-white roses, blush peonies and eucalyptus from her bouquet. Standing at the side of the wedding tent, she was able to glimpse its incredible transformation. Yards of flowing white fabric had been draped from the ceiling and adorned with rustic chandeliers, swags of greenery and string lights.

Toward the back, tables and chairs had been set up for the dinner and reception that would follow the ceremony, while what appeared to be the entire town of

Ouray now sat in the rows of white chairs at the opposite end of the tent, awaiting the bride's entrance.

The front of the tent had been left open, affording a glorious view of the mountains that backdropped the ranch. If everything went according to plan, Lily and Noah would say *I do* as the sun disappeared behind the peaks.

And there, front and center at the end of the aisle, was the arbor, repaired and upright once again, looking even more beautiful than before, draped with greenery and tiny LED lights. The perfect focal point and makeshift altar. Thanks to Jude.

She pressed a hand to her stomach, trying to quell the excitement that, at the moment, seemed a little overwhelming.

Turning, she shared a smile with the beautiful bride who, contrary to Kayla, appeared the epitome of calm. Lily looked stunning in her simple sheath dress. Since she wanted to keep things somewhat casual, she wore her long reddish-blond hair down, curled, with the sides pulled back and held by a fingertip-length lace veil that wouldn't detract from the dress.

Kayla gave her another once-over. "You are going to knock Noah's socks off."

Dressed in an ivory satin A-line dress with a deep plum sash, Lily's seven-year-old daughter, Piper, peered up at Kayla. "What does that mean?"

"It means your mommy looks gorgeous."

"You're looking pretty amazing yourself," said Lily.

Kayla bit the corner of her lipstick-covered lip. Surprisingly, she liked the way she looked, too. Especially the way her waist-length hair had been braided and twisted into a romantic low bun. Very feminine. And a far cry from her favorite overalls.

"Let's just pray I don't trip in these heels." Kayla noted her strappy nude-colored dress sandals.

They shared a giggle before Lily gave her a more serious look. "I still can't believe I'm doing this. I said I'd never marry again. Yet—" she raised a hand "—here

I am. About to walk down the aisle to the man of my dreams."

"A cowboy, no less."

Lily's smile grew wider. "And a very handsome one at that."

"You've both been through a lot." Lily had felt the sting of betrayal, and Noah's wife had passed away shortly after miscarrying their first child. "But God works in mysterious ways. I mean, who would have thought that your little vacation with the kids would lead you to this?" Kayla gestured from the ranch land outside to inside the wedding tent.

Her friend shivered with glee. "I know." She reached for Kayla's hand. "And I can't help thinking He's brought you here for a reason, too." Lily had been singing the same song ever since Kayla told her about her history with Jude.

"I agree. A new place, a new job… You've allowed me the fresh start I wanted."

Lily frowned. "That's not what I meant, and you know it."

"Lily, I'm trying to reclaim my life. For

me and my baby. The last thing I need is a man to distract me from that goal."

"Distract, no. But someone to come alongside you, partner with you, lift you up…"

In Kayla's world, that kind of man didn't exist. She'd allowed herself to be beaten down. To be taken advantage of and made into a shell of the person she once was. She wasn't about to make that mistake again.

The wedding planner interrupted them. "Ladies, it's time."

Kayla hugged her friend. "Thank you for allowing me to be a part of your special day."

Lily squeezed her. "I wouldn't have it any other way."

With notes of Elvis Presley's "Can't Help Falling in Love" flowing from an acoustic guitar, Kayla started down the aisle. Nerves continued to knot in her stomach, but she ignored them, smiling as she put one foot in front of the other.

Noah waited at the front with Jude and Colton by his side. Yet Kayla found herself fixated on Jude. How handsome he looked in his gray suit. And the smile he sent her had her stomach twisting even more. For a moment, she dared to wonder. What if she had stayed in Ouray all those years ago or even come back? Perhaps she would have walked an aisle like this, but as Jude's bride.

She looked away then, continuing to the opposite side of the altar. What was done was done. There was no going back.

After Piper took her place beside Kayla, guests stood at the sound of the wedding march. The smile on Lily's face was one of pure joy as she moved up the aisle, her eyes fixed on Noah.

Kayla couldn't help sneaking a peek at the groom. The way he looked at Lily. Had Shane ever looked at Kayla that way?

No. Yet she'd allowed herself to be fooled by his charm.

Beyond Noah, she saw Jude looking at her. Why? Had her updo come undone? Or was…?

Stupid. He would never daydream about marrying her. Nor should she entertain such notions either.

Noah met Lily when she was still several feet away, took hold of her hand and escorted her before the pastor.

"Honored guests," the pastor began, "we are here today to witness the union of Noah Stephens and Lily Davis."

Tears pricked the backs of Kayla's eyes as a lump formed in her throat. Lily was one of the sweetest people Kayla had ever known. And she so deserved to be loved and cherished. Noah was her happily-ever-after.

As the ceremony continued, the nervousness Kayla had been feeling turned to downright nausea. She sucked in a couple of deep breaths through her nose, hoping to quell the feeling. And it seemed to work. Until she handed Lily Noah's ring a short time later. Was it the heels that had her feeling so unsteady?

By the time Noah and Lily made their way up the aisle as man and wife, everything seemed to be happening in slow motion. Even the applause of the guests sounded far away.

When it was their turn to walk up the

aisle, Jude moved toward her, but her feet refused to move. They felt as though they were weighted down.

Jude stretched out his arm to take hold of her hand, his face contorting with concern. "Are you all right?"

Why did he sound like he was in a tunnel?

Suddenly, everything went black.

Worry flooded Jude's veins as he eased Kayla to the floor amid the gasps of wedding guests. He'd known she was looking kind of funny, but he never expected she'd go down. If he had, he would have gotten her out of here. Fortunately, he'd been close enough to catch her.

Kneeling beside her, he brushed the hair away from her face. Her skin was so pale.

His father came alongside him, looking as bewildered as Jude felt. "What happened?"

"I don't know any more than you do, Dad." He checked her pulse. Yes, she had one, but he couldn't concentrate long enough to give anyone a number. Instead, he was busy battling the panic threatening to break down the door of his resolve. He was a police officer. He ought to be able to handle someone passing out.

Problem was, he found himself caring way too much about this particular someone.

"We need to elevate her feet." Trent Lockridge, a family friend and doctor, stood behind Jude now. He removed his sports coat, rolled it up and placed it under Kayla's feet.

Jude quickly removed his jacket and handed it to his father, who did the same with his own coat before placing them with Trent's.

The doctor knelt opposite Jude. He checked Kayla's pulse as Noah and Lily returned.

Lily dropped beside her friend and smoothed a hand across her brow. "Kayla? Come on. Open your eyes, sweetie." Her unwavering voice reminded Jude of his mother. Calm in the midst of a storm.

Blakely Lockridge, Trent's wife, handed a medical bag to her husband, then stepped away.

Kayla moaned as the doctor pulled out his stethoscope. Rolled her head from one side to the other.

Jude lowered his head, placing his mouth next to her ear. "Wake up, Kayla. Please." He reached for her hand and gave it a squeeze as though willing her to come around.

The breath he wasn't even aware he was holding whooshed from his lungs when her eyelids fluttered open. "Thank You, God."

At first, she appeared dazed, her gaze slowly taking in her surroundings. In no time, though, her eyes widened. She tried to sit up, but Jude, Trent and Lily stopped her.

"Easy," said the doctor.

Slowly, she laid her head back. "What happened?"

"You fainted," said Jude.

"What?" She put a hand over her face. "I'm so sorry, Lily."

"For what, sweetie?" She caressed her friend's forehead.

"I ruined your wedding."

Lily smiled. "No, you didn't."

"Do you recall anything before you blacked out?" Trent continued to watch her.

Kayla seemed to think for a moment. "I remember feeling kind of queasy."

Hands resting on his thighs, the doctor seemed to evaluate the situation. "Can you tell me what you've eaten today?"

"I—I'm not sure. I had part of a cinnamon roll this morning, but I think that's it."

Trent looked from Jude to Lily. "Coupled with the pregnancy and any nervousness, that's likely the cause." He returned his focus to Kayla. "We need to get you something to eat, young lady."

When Kayla sat up, Jude took hold of her hand, wrapped his other arm around her waist and helped her to her feet. She was shaking like a leaf.

"Dad?" He looked at the man who'd remained close the entire time. Like Jude, he didn't know, nor care, what was going on with the rest of the guests. "Could you bring me the UTV, please? I'm going to take Kayla up to the ranch house for a little while."

Without asking any questions, the old man nodded before disappearing through the tent's open front.

"The house?" Kayla pouted, trying to break free, but Jude refused to let her go. "I'm supposed to be here for Lily."

"Oh, sweetie, you will be," said Lily.

Jude snugged Kayla closer. "I just want you to have a few minutes to recover without everyone looking at you."

"I know you're right, but—" Tears welled in her eyes.

Trying to keep things light, he said, "If you cry, you're going to ruin your makeup."

She tilted her head back, blinking. "Yeah, and Lily paid big bucks for it."

"The makeup?" He looked from Lily to Kayla.

"She hired a professional."

Lily shrugged. "A special day deserves

special treatment." She reached for her friend's hand. "Right now, though, I want you to do as Jude says. Take a little time-out. Eat something. And then come back here when you're ready. Okay?"

Kayla nodded, albeit reluctantly.

Dad appeared outside the tent just then. He hopped out of the still-running utility vehicle to rejoin them. "It's all yours, son." He turned his attention to Kayla. "We'll take care of things out here. You concentrate on yourself and that baby."

Her smile was a tremulous one. "Yes, sir."

Jude helped her into the utility vehicle, then drove the short distance to the house, welcoming both the fresh air and momentary reprieve from the chaos. He shoved a hand through his hair. Thank God she was all right. And he prayed the baby was, too.

When they reached the house, Jude again assisted her, up the steps, through the mudroom and into the kitchen. At least she seemed a little steadier.

Once she settled into a chair at the table, he took a quick inventory of available foods. "What are you hungry for?" He opened the refrigerator and peered inside.

"That's the problem, I'm not hungry."

Still holding on to the door, he eyed her over his shoulder. "What would be good for the baby, then?"

Her pretty lips pressed together.

Closing the door, he moved to stand beside her, crossing his arms over his chest for maximum effect as he looked down at her. "You heard the doctor. Even if you're not hungry, that little one growing inside of you probably is. What do you think he or she might like?"

Her expression relaxed then, the corners of her mouth tilting slightly upward.

"We've got sandwich makings, cookies, some lasagna from last night—"

"How about a glass of milk?"

At least it had protein. And babies spent

their first few months eating—make that drinking—nothing but milk, so that oughta do.

"I can do that." He grabbed a glass from the cupboard and filled it before joining her at the table.

She took a sip. "It's not like I was purposely starving myself. I was just busy, that's all." One shoulder lifted. "And I kind of forgot to eat."

Leaning forward in one of the wooden chairs, he rested his forearms on his thighs and clasped his hands. "I understand. But when you're eating for two, you can't afford to do that."

"Guess I learned that the hard way." She rubbed her belly. "Sorry, little one." Glancing at Jude, she said, "Actually, I've been looking forward to that filet mignon they're serving tonight. And the cake, of course."

"Well, as soon as you're feeling better, we'll head back out there so you can get some real food."

"And cake?" The teasing lilt of her brow told him she was feeling better.

"And cake."

After another swig of milk, she slumped against the back of the chair. "Thank you for fixing the arbor."

"It looked pretty good up there, didn't it?"

"I think it was the star of the show." She fingered the rim of her glass. "Second only to Lily and Noah."

Funny, he was thinking the same thing about Kayla. While she was always beautiful, this softer side of her was… Wow! Between the hair, the dress and the makeup, she was the prettiest thing he'd ever laid eyes on.

As he continued to watch her, her smile suddenly disappeared. She set a hand to her belly.

"Kayla? What is it?" He moved beside her. "Are you okay?" Had her passing out done something to the baby?

Her expression morphed into one of surprise. "Yeah. It's——" She faced him, her chestnut eyes suddenly alight with something he'd never seen before. "I think I just felt the baby move." She placed her other hand beside the first, her smile growing wide. "There it is again."

Watching her, he couldn't help smiling, too. "He or she must have liked the milk."

"This is amazing." She reached for his hand and pressed it against her protruding belly. "Do you feel it?"

He hesitated at first, wanting to pull away, but not wanting to hurt her feelings. Then he felt it. The slightest kick beneath his fingers.

His own eyes widened. "You might have a punter in there."

She set her hand next to his. "Or a soccer player."

Looking into Kayla's eyes, with both of their hands resting over her growing child, he wasn't sure he'd ever experienced a more precious or intimate moment in his life. He silently thanked God for allowing him to share this incredible experience with her, the gift of life. And as he watched her, one thing became perfectly clear.

He would do everything in his power to protect Kayla and her baby.

Chapter Nine

Kayla stepped onto the front porch of Granger House Inn the next morning, feeling more than a little embarrassed about all that had transpired last night. As if fainting wasn't bad enough, she'd practically forced Jude to feel her baby move. Why would he care? It wasn't his child. Yet that hadn't stopped her from grabbing his hand and pressing it against her stomach, no matter how reluctant he'd been.

She shook her head. How stupid could she be?

The cool morning air sent a shiver through her as she continued down the wooden steps. Oddly enough, though,

Jude had stayed by her side the rest of the night. And the way he held her in his arms as they danced... It had been a long time since she'd felt so safe.

Something she couldn't let happen again. Since Shane's death, her goal had been to rediscover her self-confidence. And while she might have stumbled last week while she and Jude were building the arbor, she had to keep moving forward. Because never again would she allow herself to fall under the control of someone else.

Jude's not Shane.

No, he was not. She puffed out a laugh, remembering the way he'd called her out during one of her meltdowns. Even asking her what had happened to her confidence. Which meant she had to guard herself all the more or risk losing her heart. Especially now that she was on her way to the ranch.

Drawing in a bolstering breath, she climbed into her truck. Aside from general cleanup, the event team was due back at ten to break everything down. So, whether she wanted to or not, she pulled out of Carly's drive just before nine thirty.

North of town, she glimpsed the winding waters of the Uncompahgre River to her left. Now that the wedding was over, it was time for her to find a new norm. To begin her new life. Something that could start with making plans to move into the house Lily had reserved for her. Livie's House, she'd called it.

Since Lily and Noah had decided to take a more practical approach to their honeymoon and were returning to Denver to start the process of emptying her house, they'd be bringing back some of Kayla's stuff. Which meant she might be able to move in as soon as this weekend, assuming that worked for Andrew and Carly.

Kayla could also start checking into permits. Every county had its own set of regulations, she just needed to find out what the requirements were in Ouray and go from there.

She also needed to set up an appointment with an obstetrician.

Hmm. Seemed she had more to do than she thought. She'd best start a list when she returned to the bed-and-breakfast.

Pulling up the drive at the ranch, she noticed that the big white box truck from the rental company was already there and the tent had disappeared. She glanced at the clock on her dash. No, she wasn't late.

Jude met her at the front of the deck as she got out of her truck. "What are you doing here?"

"I came to help clean up." She eyed the truck at the back of the house. "They're early."

"Got here about an hour ago." His dark gaze never left her. "How are you feeling?"

"Much better." Uneasy under his scrutiny, she walked in the direction of the workers. "They weren't supposed to be here until ten."

"They probably wanted to get it out of the way so they could enjoy their Sunday." He matched her steps, gravel crunching beneath their booted feet as he continued to study her. "I hope you ate something this morning."

"As a matter of fact—"

"And I mean more than just a bite."

"Actually—" slowing, she sent him a perturbed look "—I took full advantage of Carly's breakfast spread. I had eggs, sausage, muffins and fruit."

His slow smile had her quickly looking away. "Good."

She stopped at the far end of the shop and scanned the open pasture, noting only the workers from the rental company. "Where is everyone?"

"Dad and Hillary took Colton and Piper to Sunday school. And I'm assuming Daniel went on to church, too."

"How did the kids do last night?" Clint was keeping Lily's children while she and Noah were in Denver.

"They were fine. Though it'll be interesting to see how the old man does when he has to get them off to school tomorrow. That particular job always belonged to Mama."

Sorrow leached into Kayla's heart. "I'm sorry about Mona. She was one of the most kindhearted yet strongest women I ever knew. I know how much you all loved her."

"Yeah, made things kinda rough." He rocked back on the heels of his well-worn cowboy boots. "We've adjusted, though. Dad's got Hillary."

"I like her. She seems very nice."

He nodded. "She's good for Dad. Keeps him on his toes."

Kayla buried her hands in the pockets of her overalls, welcoming the sun's warmth on her back. "Looks like it's just you and me for cleanup detail then, huh?" Something she hadn't anticipated.

"Nope. We took care of everything earlier, before the truck arrived. Not that there was that much." He pointed toward the workers. "These guys will get the rest."

So, while she was killing time stuffing her face, Jude and his family were doing the job she should have been doing. "Why didn't you let me know you were doing the cleanup first?" She couldn't help the annoyance in her voice as she faced him. "I could have come earlier."

"I know." He shrugged. "But I figured you needed the rest."

Her gaze narrowed. "For your information, I don't appreciate being coddled. My doctor says I can continue doing the same things I did before."

"I believe you. However, when was the last time you passed out? You could at least give yourself a day to recover."

"I'm fine, Jude." Her exasperation wasn't nearly as heartfelt as she wanted it to be. "I don't need you telling me what I can and cannot do."

"Sue me for caring." For a second she thought she'd hurt his feelings. Then he said, "I do have a suggestion, though."

"And what might that be?"

Turning, he eyed the men loading the truck. "Winter will be here before we know it." He looked at her now. "Since this is such a pretty day, I thought it might be worth a drive up Last Dollar Road. We could check out the fall color. Catch some views of Mount Wilson and Dallas Divide."

"They might even have snow by now." Oops. Seemed the unwanted excitement that bubbled inside of her at the thought of spending time in the mountains refused to be contained. "Or not." She toed at the ground.

"You were probably right the first time."

She kept her eyes glued to the ground, not wanting to see the satisfied grin she heard in his voice.

"Of course, we'd have to wait until these guys leave. But if you're interested, we could pack a lunch and make a day of it."

Brow lifting in a gotcha sort of manner, she looked at him. "What about my recovery?"

His hands moved to his hips as he glowered. "You'll be riding in the passenger seat. *Maybe* doing a little walking. It's not like we'll be scaling Mount Sneffels." He paused then. Briefly looked away. "But if you'd prefer to go back to the bed-and-breakfast—"

"I didn't say that." She groaned inside. Did she have to sound so eager?

I thought you wanted to keep your distance from Jude.

She did. But it had been so long since she'd been in the mountains. Especially the San Juans. And Last Dollar Road was so pretty this time of year. It was one of the last places Jude had taken her before she and her parents left Ouray.

You could drive yourself.

True. But after suffering a flat tire and a dead battery all in the same week, she wasn't sure she wanted to risk it. Which left her with two options. Spend the afternoon with Jude or go back to Granger House Inn.

"Come on, Kayla." He nudged her with his elbow, the way he used to all those years ago. Whenever he was trying to talk her into something. "It'll be fun."

That's what she was afraid of.

Memories invaded her mind. Thoughts of happier times. When there was a man who made her feel loved, wanted and safe.

When life was easy and she didn't have a care in the world.

But that was a long time ago. Now she'd been misleading Jude, blaming her erratic behavior on stress and the wedding, instead of telling him the truth about her marriage.

Looking up at his handsome face, she knew he deserved her honesty. What she didn't know was if she could bring herself to tell him. Not when letting him believe a lie was so much easier.

Jude had a feeling that getting Kayla out of Ouray, away from the ranch and all the hubbub of this past week, would do her a world of good. And seeing the contentment on her face as she stared out over the rolling hills blanketed with shades of orange and gold, he knew his impromptu suggestion had been a good one.

The autumn air was cool but not cold, and beyond the colorful foliage, the snow-dusted peaks of Mount Wilson glistened in the distance.

"I told you there'd be snow." She grinned over her shoulder.

Or not, he was tempted to remind her. But he chose to let it slide. "Yeah, you called it, all right."

"I've missed having the mountains so close." Hands perched on the backs of her hips, she turned from the view to him and back again. "I think it's funny how everybody associates Denver with mountains. Yet while you can see them, it takes a while to get there." She swept an arm through the air. "Out here, everything is so close."

"Yep, sometimes, all you have to do is walk out your back door."

Her laughter was a sweet sound. "This is true. Especially if you live in Ouray proper."

"Which you're about to do."

"I know." Her head moved from side to side, her long ponytail swaying with each movement. "I still can't believe it." She sent him a somewhat befuddled look. "And here I thought I was just coming to Ouray for a wedding."

"Speaking of the wedding..." He walked the few feet to his truck and lowered the tailgate. "Care to join me for some lunch? Those roast beef sandwiches are calling my name." Moving to the side of the vehicle, he opened the back door and retrieved the box they'd loaded with chips, leftover wedding cake and, of course, sandwiches.

"How did you get lunch out of wedding?" She snagged a small bag of cheese puffs from the box and pushed herself up onto the tailgate.

He chuckled as she popped the bag open and began crunching. "Simple. We have wedding cake for dessert."

"Dessert?" She shoved another puff into her mouth. "I'm thinking appetizer."

Watching her now, seeing her shoulders relax, enjoying the banter... This was what he'd hoped to achieve when he invited her to join him.

"I don't think I've ever seen such a beautiful place." She licked her fingertips that now matched the orange leaves below them. "And I've seen a lot of places. But these colors..." Once again, she took in the brilliant aspens. "They're so vibrant."

"You'll get no argument from me." Pulling his sandwich from its plastic bag, he continued, "This is one of my favorite places to come in the fall." He took a hearty bite, the flavors of beef and horseradish making him eager for the next mouthful.

"I can certainly see why." Wadding her empty cheese puff bag, Kayla let go a contented sigh. "Thank you for sharing it with me."

There's nobody I'd rather share it with. The thought had him choking, though he covered by taking a sip of water from the one of the bottles from the box. Then he grabbed a second sandwich and handed it to Kayla. "Here. Protein before cake."

Instantly, her eyes narrowed, her lips pressing tightly together. She glared at him, then at the sandwich before accepting it, as though she found it appalling that someone would care about her well-being and that of her child. And he would give anything to know why.

After another bite, he mustered his courage. "May I ask you something?"

Continuing to take in the view, she ate, never looking his way. "Depends what it is."

No point backing down now. Even if she didn't answer, at least she'd know what was on his mind.

"Why do you get so defensive whenever you *think* I'm trying to tell you what to do?"

Her chewing slowed, her shoulders again becoming rigid as she lowered her sandwich to her lap and swallowed. "Well, for the past two years a good part of my life has been out of my control. Now I'm trying to regain some semblance of normalcy, and you're interfering with that goal."

Just like that first day at the hotel, her words flew all over him. "Interfere? How could you possibly believe that? I mean, sure, it's been a long time, but I'm not that kind of person and you know it."

After a long stretch of silence, she straightened. "Let's just say my perception has been skewed."

"How?"

More silence, and he could tell she was debating whether or not to divulge whatever it was she was clinging to so tightly.

Finally, she blew out a long breath laced with resignation. "My husband died at the hands of a drunk driver."

He wasn't sure how that applied, but he was shocked nonetheless. "That's rough. I don't know why people think they can get behind the wheel—"

"He was the one who was drunk." She looked at him now, a mixture of fear and relief etching creases into her brow. "Shane was an alcoholic. But I didn't learn that until after we were married." Pausing, she seemed to ponder what or how much to tell him. "He got drunk the first night of our honeymoon in Cabo San Lucas. Then spent the entire evening voicing his regret over marrying me and telling me how blessed I was to have him."

Jude's sandwich soured in his stomach. "What kind of guy does that?"

"One who doesn't remember it in the morning. And on the off chance that he does, he goes out of his way to apologize and atone for whatever he did."

His gaze searched hers. "This went on your entire marriage?"

"He had stretches where he wouldn't drink at all. I used to pray he would stay sober because he was…*different* when he drank." She looked away. "But, for him, alcohol was a convincing mistress. One I couldn't begin to compete with."

Jude was almost afraid to ask, but he had to know. "Did he ever hurt you?" Her silence spoke volumes, and his anger flashed. Yet he managed to keep his breathing even.

Just when he thought he couldn't stand it anymore, she said, "Things got progressively worse that last year. Lily advised me to leave him—"

"But you didn't." He knew his reaction was probably harsher than she deserved right now, but he'd been called to domestic situations before and had very distinct opinions.

"I made a vow." Determined eyes bored into his, as though willing him to understand.

"Is that why you're still wearing your wedding ring?"

She glanced at the plain gold band. "Not really. I simply wanted to avoid the whole unwed and pregnant persona." After a brief pause, she continued, "For two years I clung to the hope that Shane would change. Until one night in May."

"What happened?"

"He came in late. Drunk, of course. And when I refused his advances…" She eyed the jagged peaks in the distance. "Things got a little rough."

"What do you mean by rough?"

"We argued. I tried to leave." She looked away. "And he…did whatever he had to to stop me."

Anger propelled Jude off the tailgate. He paced as a wind kicked up, sending a chill down his spine. The thought of that slime-ball treating Kayla like that disgusted Jude in a way he'd never experienced before. He wanted to let out a guttural yell or punch something. But there was no way he'd do that in front of Kayla. Not now, not ever.

"I knew then that I had to get out." She lifted a shoulder. "So, I talked to Lily, and she offered me a place to stay. I was just waiting until I knew I could break away without him finding out, but before I was able to make that move, he was dead."

He stopped in front of her, taking care to keep his voice even. "Did you ever tell anyone, besides Lily, about the abuse?"

She lowered head. "I was too ashamed."

"Kayla, I—"

"Don't say it, Jude." Hands clasped, she picked at her fingernails. "I don't want you to feel sorry for me. What happened is in the past. Now I'm getting a do-over. I only told you because—"

"I asked." And he was grateful she trusted him enough to tell him the truth.

"I need you to understand that I'm not that carefree girl you once knew. I've been through a lot." Her hand fell to her swollen belly. "I'm older and, hopefully, wiser."

Again, curiosity prodded his brain. And since he was on a roll... "When did you find out you were pregnant?"

She looked away for a moment. "About a month after Shane passed. I thought I was just stressed, but I went to the doctor and... Well, you know the rest."

Looking into her sad eyes, he wanted to pull her into his arms and hold her until all of those bad memories disappeared from her mind. That wasn't going to happen, though. Even if he tried, she'd only push him away. That kind of healing could only come from God. And how he prayed God would heal her.

Despite the war raging inside of him, he managed to hold on to the appearance of control. "You say you're no longer that carefree girl. But unlike the past, we don't know what the future holds. Perhaps she'll, one day, make an appearance again." The way she had only a few moments ago, before he stirred this hornets' nest. And he'd give anything to be there when that happened.

Chapter Ten

Kayla would kill for a supreme pizza with extra cheese.

Instead, she dropped onto her bed at Granger House Inn late Wednesday afternoon and tore open the package of peanut butter crackers she'd snagged from her snack stash in the top drawer of the dresser. Despite indulging in her favorite Mexican fast food before leaving Montrose an hour and a half ago, she was starving.

Biting into the first little sandwich, she grabbed her purse from the end of the bed and pulled out the small stack of brochures she'd received at her new obstetricians' office. There was information on the hospital, some coupons for baby formula and diapers and...

She singled out the flyer adorned with a teddy bear.

Childbirth classes.

Her baby wasn't even due for another three and a half months. Of course, with the holidays thrown in there...

Shoving what was left of the cracker into her mouth, she flipped the brochure over to look at upcoming class dates.

She skimmed the information until a single phrase captured her attention.

Price per couple.

Kayla was not a couple, nor was she even half of a couple. She was flying solo. Headed down this scary path to parenthood all by herself. The last thing she wanted was be the only single in a classroom full of couples.

Her doctor had told her not to worry, that all she needed was a coach. Someone she trusted to encourage her and be there for her during labor and delivery.

At a time like this, most women might

turn to their mothers. But Claudette Brennan had already made it clear that, while she loved her daughter, she had no desire to witness the birth of her first, and likely only, grandchild. She was happy to wait until both mother and child were out of the delivery room.

That didn't leave Kayla with many options. There were only two people in Ouray she trusted—Lily and Jude. And there was no way she was going to ask Jude to be her birthing coach. She'd simply have to mention it to Lily once she returned from her honeymoon.

And while her friend would, no doubt, be more than happy to take on the role, now that Lily was married, Kayla felt bad asking her to be on call at all hours in those weeks leading up to the delivery. Lily had a family of her own to take care of.

For the briefest of moments, Kayla found herself wishing Shane was still alive. At least then she wouldn't be facing this dilemma. He would be her coach. That was, *if* he showed up for the classes. And was sober enough to drive her to the hospital when she went into labor.

A shiver sifted through her, and she crawled under the cozy comforter. She didn't even want to think about what it would have been like to raise a child in the toxic environment that had been her marriage. She wanted her baby to grow up knowing he or she was loved uncondi- tionally, in a home where they were free to be themselves, not forced to conform to the whims of someone who had a distorted view of love.

She tugged the comforter to her chin and closed her eyes. *God, there have been so many changes in my life these past several months. Things I don't really understand. But thank You for protecting my baby.*

A gentle rap sounded at her door.

"Kayla?" Carly whispered on the other side.

Kayla tossed the covers off her and moved across the plush carpet in her sock feet to open the door.

Smiling, Carly said, "I was afraid you might be napping."

Kayla clung to the glass doorknob, her mind still reeling from all the twists and turns her life had taken since May. She'd never been a fan of roller coasters, but at least she could take solace in knowing that God was at the controls. "No, just resting."

"Good, because you have a guest."

She darted a glance toward the steps. "Anyone I know?"

"Jude," Carly tossed over her shoulder, already heading back downstairs.

Jude? Now?

Ducking back inside her room, Kayla checked her look in the mirror. Thanks to Carly, she now had clothes that actually fit her expanding waistline. And the black maternity leggings and pale gray tunic were a nice change from her overalls.

Not that she should care. It was only Jude, after all. The man she'd revealed her deepest, darkest secret to three days ago and hadn't seen or heard from since.

She'd begun to think he was avoiding

her. Believing her weak for remaining in an abusive relationship.

She grabbed a brush and ran it through her hair. Well, he could judge all he wanted. It was easy to do, until you found yourself someplace you never thought you'd be. Which was why, aside from Lily and now Jude, no one else knew the truth about her marriage and Shane. Not even Shane's parents.

Her insides twisted. She had yet to inform her in-laws of her decision to stay in Ouray. No doubt they'd try to talk her out of it. Which was precisely why she'd been putting it off. Perhaps she'd wait until she moved into Livie's House.

After tugging on her boots, she made her way downstairs, through the Victorian-style parlor and into the dining room, where she spotted Jude just inside the kitchen, holding baby Lucas. The sight halted her steps. She paused beside the antique sideboard, blinking away tears. The tenderness in his voice as he talked to the babe and the loving look in his eyes…

She wrapped her arms around her midsection. Her child would never know the love of a father. Wouldn't experience the kind of special bond Kayla had shared with her dad. Her insides clenched. Oh, how she missed him.

Tilting her head back, she continued to blink. Why were all these things she'd never even considered before bombarding her today? Her pregnancy was just as real now as it had been weeks ago when she was still in Denver.

Her hand fell to her belly. But back then, she hadn't felt her baby move yet. Or seen it sucking its tiny thumb, the way it had today when the doctor did the sonogram. Now this life that had been growing inside of her for months seemed more real than ever. And yet as terrifying as it may seem, she could hardly wait to meet him or her. Meaning she could *not* give in to the fear all these things rattling through her brain tried to evoke. Instead, she had to trust God to give her the strength and wherewithal to be everything her child needed her to be.

With a bolstering breath, she continued into Carly's beautiful white kitchen. "Hello, Jude."

"There you are." Standing at the large, marble-topped island, he smiled at Kayla before passing Lucas into Carly's waiting arms.

"Come on, little fella." Carly laid her son against her shoulder. "You and I have a date to fold some laundry."

The two disappeared into the adjoining family room, where a television played as Jude's cautious gaze moved from Kayla's face to her feet and back again. "Everything all right?" His scrutiny had her feeling rather self-conscious.

She studied her barely there fingernails. "Why wouldn't it be?"

One broad shoulder lifted. "I just wanted to make sure. Sorry, I didn't get by earlier. It's been a busy week with work and trying to catch up on my orders."

Her cheeks heated as she recalled her little pity party upstairs. She moved across the dark hardwood floor to the window, hoping he wouldn't notice. Of course he'd been busy. Between helping her with the arbor, the wedding and their drive up to Last Dollar Sunday afternoon, Jude had sacrificed a lot of time last week. Yet she'd thought he was avoiding her. Stupid.

Even if he was, it shouldn't matter. Not to her anyway. Lily was her friend, too, and Kayla didn't get all bent out of shape when she didn't hear from *her.*

"That's all right. I've been kind of busy myself."

"Doing what?" He sounded surprised.

"Researching permits for the hotel." She faced him again, annoyance at his incredulity jolting her composure back into place. "Today I had a doctor's appointment and even did a little shopping."

"Picking out stuff for the baby?" A smile played at the corners of his mouth.

"No. Though I suppose I should start thinking about that."

"Maybe once you have your own place again you can focus on that." Hands tucked in the pockets of his jeans, he moved closer. "Baby doing okay?" His seemingly genuine concern for her child never failed to reach past her defenses, softening even the hardest parts of her heart.

"The doctor says he or she is doing just fine."

"Sounds like something worth celebrating to me." He looked at her with those dark eyes that once had the power to take her breath away. "Do you have any dinner plans?"

Sort of. But they involved lots of melted mozzarella, not Jude. "Um—"

"Because I could really go for some pizza."

Her gaze jerked to his. "Did you just say pizza?"

"I did. There's a new place here in town that I've been dying to try. Word has it that they make their dough fresh every day."

Her mouth watered. "That does sound good." And it was exactly what she'd been craving. How could Jude have known that, though?

Well, at least she now knew where to go for pizza. But dinner with Jude when her emotions had been so off the rails?

"Besides, you look like you could use a friend."

She straightened. "What's that supposed to mean?"

"Nothing bad. You just look—" he shrugged "—I don't know, a little over-whelmed."

Since when had Jude Stephens turned into a mind reader? First the pizza, now he could tell she was overwhelmed? She really needed to learn to hide her feelings better.

"You have a habit of looking at your hands when you're stressed."

Still staring at him, she moved her hands behind her back. Maybe he wasn't a mind reader, but knowing he watched her that closely, analyzed her movements—

"And before you go getting all offended,

remember that I'm a cop. I'm supposed to be able to read people's body language."

That did not reassure her. Now she was going to be aware of every little movement she made, wondering what he might read into it.

"About that dinner, though." He stepped away. "I also hear this place has some garlic knots that are pretty amazing."

Did the man know how to drive his point home or what?

"All right, already." She started for the door. "I'll get my jacket."

Jude moved down the front walk of Granger House with Kayla by his side, feeling like a grade-A jerk. She'd finally opened up to him, sharing something deeply painful. And yet he'd waited three days to contact her again. Sure, he'd been busy, but he could have called or texted to see how she was doing.

But he hadn't. And from the moment he laid eyes on her in Carly's kitchen, he knew something was troubling her. Now he could only pray he could get her to open up again and tell him what was wrong.

What if you're the problem? Maybe she thinks your silence was because of what she told you.

Why would she think that?

You were kind of hard on her.

No, he wasn't. Hands tucked in the pockets of his jacket, he eyed the woman walking silently beside him. Okay, maybe a little. But it wasn't her he was frustrated with. It was that jerk, Shane. She understood that. Didn't she?

Approaching his truck, he said, "Would you prefer to walk or ride?"

"Let's walk." She gave a half smile. "That way, I can justify eating an entire pizza by walking some of it off on the way home."

He peered down at her. "That's some weird logic. But since you're the one who's pregnant, I'm not going to argue." Touching her elbow, he guided her down the sidewalk. "Besides, our nice weather may not hold out much longer. I heard talk of snow this weekend."

"Snow?" Her chestnut eyes were wide. "Good thing I picked up some new boots today."

"Speaking of today, tell me about your doctor appointment."

She shrugged. "He said everything's still on track. Baby's healthy."

"That's good."

She looked up at him. "Were you worried?"

"With all the stress you've been under and then fainting, yeah, I was concerned."

She continued to watch him. As though surprised. "In that case, you'll be happy to know that he even did a sonogram."

"Could he tell if it was a boy or a girl?"

"Probably, but I told him I didn't want to know."

He wanted to ask her why, but it was her decision. No matter how curious he might be. "You never peeked at any of your Christmas presents early, did you?"

"Of course not." Her brow puckered.

"That would totally ruin the surprise." The corners of her mouth lifted then. "You did, though. Didn't you?"

He couldn't help grinning and was glad to see Kayla relaxing. "Maybe."

She shook her head. "I'll tell you what I did see in the sonogram."

"What's that?"

"The baby was sucking its thumb. Had its little fist up to its mouth… Just about the cutest thing I've ever seen."

"Won't be long and you'll be holding him or her."

She blew out a breath, her enthusiasm waning a notch. "I know."

Touching her arm, he stopped. "I thought you'd be excited about that."

"I am. Sort of. And I'll be fine, it's just…" Her shoulder lifted. "Suddenly it's all becoming so real. I'm going to be a mother. Like, 100 percent responsible for another human being." Her eyes slowly traveled to his, as though searching for answers. "What if I mess up?"

"I'm pretty sure just about everyone

who's ever had a baby in the history of the world has asked that same question."

"I'm serious, Jude. Babies aren't like power tools. They don't come with a user manual." He could almost feel her angst.

"Sorry, I was only trying to say that what you're feeling is normal. And as for the user manual, my grandmother would have said that the Bible was the only guidebook we need, no matter what the circumstance." He stepped closer, rubbing her upper arms with his hands. "I get that you're scared, but you've got two things going for you that I *know* will make you the best mother ever."

Skepticism pinched her expression as she peered up at him through long lashes. "And those are…?"

"Common sense. And a heart filled with more love than that baby will be able to handle."

She turned away, but not before he saw the sheen in her eyes. Nodded. "You know, if I don't get some pizza pretty quick, I just might keel over."

"Well now, we can't have that." He reached for her hand and aimed for Main Street. "Come on."

He held open the door to the pizza place and allowed Kayla to enter first. As with many of Ouray's restaurants, this one had gone through many incarnations. Everything from fine dining to, now, a pizza joint. He could only hope that it lived up to all the hype he'd heard from locals and, if it did, that it would stick around for a while.

Inside, the aromas of fresh-baked bread and garlic awakened his appetite. Fortunately, they were seated right away and the waiter promptly dropped off a basket of garlic knots before taking their order.

Kayla knew exactly what she wanted, a supreme pizza with extra cheese, while he vacillated between the all-meat and the straight pepperoni, ultimately deciding on the all-meat.

Tearing into a garlic knot, he watched the steam rise from the warm roll.

"These are amazing." Kayla's voice was

muffled by the bite she'd already taken. "Definitely fwesh."

"Didn't your mother ever tell you not to talk with your mouth full?"

She swallowed, then sent him a satisfied grin. "Trust me, it wasn't anywhere near full."

He laughed before sampling the piece he'd broken off. At least she was smiling.

"Those are some good rolls, ain't they?"

Jude turned at the sound of his father's voice to see the man approaching with Hillary at his side. Seemed the two of them were together more than they were apart lately. And that was okay. Dad was only in his midsixties, and Jude liked Hillary. If they made each other happy, then more power to them.

"Can't argue with you there." Jude held up the other half of his garlic knot.

"They're delicious." Kayla reached for a second, eyeing the couple. "Would you two like to join us?" She motioned to the two empty chairs at their table.

"Oh, no, that's all right, hon." Hillary waved a hand. "We're on our way out anyway."

Arms crossed and resting atop the table, Kayla leaned closer. "So, is the pizza as good everyone says?"

Hillary peered left, then right before stooping almost secretively toward Kayla. "Even better."

Kayla's face lit up. "Hot dog!"

Hillary's smile widened. "Looks like somebody's got a craving."

Tearing off a piece of her roll, Kayla said, "You have no idea."

"Oh, I believe I do." The older woman winked.

Dad nudged Jude's shoulder. "Don't forget, we're working cattle first thing tomorrow."

Jude's insides twisted. He didn't have time for working cattle. Not when he had orders coming in regularly from repeat customers, pleased with the quality of his work. And he still had work to do for the project in Telluride. Yet he'd scheduled the day off, not so he could catch up on his work, but to work cattle. All because Jude couldn't seem to bring himself to tell his father the truth.

He had to correct that tomorrow.

"I haven't forgotten." How could he when the man kept reminding him?

The waiter arrived with their pizzas just then.

"Clint, we need to leave these two to their supper." Hillary smoothed a hand across Jude's father's back, as though encouraging him to move along.

"Good to see you again, Kayla." Dad waved.

"Bye." She smiled as they departed, then eagerly grabbed a piece of her pizza. "This smells *so* good."

"Yeah. It does." Though Jude's hunger had been replaced with angst. How would the old man take the news? Would he get mad or understand? For the most part, his father was a reasonable fellow. Occasionally he just needed time to come around to someone else's way of thinking, but there were other times when he allowed his pride to stand in the way of common sense. Jude had witnessed it firsthand when his father and his brother Matt ended up estranged for years. Until Dad swallowed his pride and acknowledged he'd been in the wrong.

That was a tough time for Matt. And Jude did not want to go down that road.

"You haven't touched your pizza." Kayla, on the other hand, had already scarfed down two slices of hers.

He glanced down at his hand-tossed meaty pizza. "Sorry. I guess I was lost in thought."

"Uh-huh." She wiped her hands on a white paper napkin, her gaze fixed on him. "And I'm guessing it has something to do with your dad."

He picked up a slice and set it on his plate. "What makes you think that?"

"Because your entire expression changed as soon as he mentioned working cattle."

She could see that?

"What gives?"

"It's nothing. I just hated taking another day off work, that's all."

Leaning back in her chair, she folded her hands on her belly. "Sorry, that doesn't work for me."

"What doesn't?"

Her gaze narrowed. "I don't appreciate being lied to."

And he had lied. Blatantly. As if that would earn him her trust.

But she already had so much on her plate. He didn't want to burden her with his problems.

Still, she had opened up to him. If he hoped to build any kind of relationship with her, it was time for him to do the same.

"I'm sorry, Kayla. I shouldn't have disrespected you like that." He surveyed the space around them, relieved to find it empty. Ouray was a small town where word could travel faster than a wildfire.

Returning his focus to Kayla, he said, "My father wants—make that expects—me to take over his cattle business."

Her expression turned to one of confusion. "But you don't like cattle ranching. Or you didn't used to anyway."

"You remembered." And for some reason, that surprised him.

"There are a lot of things I remember, Jude. So, what do your brothers have to say about that news?"

"They don't know. Nobody does, except me and my father." He eyed the untouched pizza on his plate. "Which puts me in an even tighter spot. I don't want to disappoint him, but my business is finally at a point where I'm ready to quit the police department to focus on woodworking full-time."

Grabbing a third slice, Kayla said, "I don't suppose you could do both, could you? Cattle ranching and woodworking?"

"Running two businesses? You obviously overestimate me."

Her smile warmed him. "Well, I know what your mother would tell you to do."

He waited.

"She'd tell you to pray about it."

"I have been."

"And?"

"If I do what I feel like I've been called to do, I'll end up hurting my father. But I don't want to give up my dream either." He let go a frustrated sigh. "I just wish the old man could be proud of me."

"Jude, I'm sure your father will be proud of you whatever you choose. I also know that if God has called you to something, He will pave the way. But you can't keep your dad hanging. You need to tell him."

"I know. And it looks like I'll be doing it tomorrow."

Chapter Eleven

In the storage room of the barn the next morning, Jude finished gathering all of the medicines and automatic syringes he and his father would need. Aside from vaccinating the cattle, they'd be evaluating the animals' overall health and sorting out those that were younger or thinner and moving them to a separate pasture where they could be given adequate food to help sustain them through the winter months.

When Jude was a kid, he always looked forward to helping his father, having a little one-on-one time with him. Whether it was checking the herd, feeding, fixing fences or working cattle, he just wanted to be with his dad. Spring, summer, fall or winter, he was by his father's side. He knew every aspect of running a cattle ranch.

But he wasn't passionate about it. Not like his father.

No, Jude's passion was wood. From the moment he got his first pocketknife at age seven, he'd been whittling and carving. Then, when he was in high school, he went to the house of a friend whose father had a wood shop. That opened up a whole new world. He'd find excuses to go over there just so he could watch the man create furniture, spindles and even decorative bowls.

Suddenly, any money Jude made went toward buying carving tools, chisels, routers and, of course, wood. Eventually, he cleared out a corner of his parents' shed, which, until then, had mostly been used for storing tools, lawn equipment and snowmobiles.

Intrigued by all of the intricate millwork on the many Victorian homes in Ouray, he went to work for a guy who was renovating one of the most gingerbread-laden houses in town. Not only was it where Jude met Kayla, but it was also where he discovered what it was he wanted to do with the rest of his life.

Now he was finding a certain measure of success in his custom and reproduction work and was prepared to give up his day job and focus solely on woodworking. But his father was oblivious to Jude's desires. And, somehow, he had to find a way to make the man understand.

After double-checking to make sure he had everything, Jude exited the barn and continued around to the pens at the back of the building.

Gray skies overhead and a definitive chill in the air had him admitting it was good that they were working the cattle today. Because, from the looks of things, winter could be headed their way anytime. Snow was already in the higher elevations and with this upcoming cold snap, anything was possible.

And to think, it had been so pleasant yesterday. Even as he walked Kayla back to Granger House Inn after dinner last night, the star-filled skies had been clear and the still air just cool enough to warrant a light jacket. Matter of fact, it had been so pleasant that, once they'd reached their destination, they'd settled on the porch swing and talked for at least an hour.

Seemed impending motherhood was attempting to get the best of Kayla. Thoughts of childbirth and being a single parent threatened to overwhelm her. Later, as they discussed things the baby might need, he made the mistake of pulling up a list of recommended baby items on his phone, which only added to her angst. Who'd have thought that babies required so much gear? Of course, a lot of it wouldn't be needed until the baby was a few months old, but he'd still had to talk Kayla off the ledge. Assure her that she had plenty of time.

By the time he returned to the ranch last night, he'd decided that he wanted to make her a crib. Not only would it save her from having to purchase one, a handcrafted crib would be an heirloom. And he could make it whatever style she liked. Besides, he wanted to do something special for her. After all she'd been through, she deserved it. And so much more.

He rounded the corner as his father and a couple of neighboring ranchers finished driving the cattle into the large pen at the back of the barn. Normally, Noah would have helped them, too, but since he was on his honeymoon...

Over the next few hours, they saw to the needs of each and every cow. Some were released back into the main pasture while others were loaded into a trailer so they could be moved to a separate pasture.

"Appreciate the help, fellas." A favor Dad would repay, because that was just the way ranchers did things. Dad closed the gate on the trailer after the last cow had been loaded.

"Our pleasure." While his son loaded their horses, Jim Osborn nudged his cowboy hat with a gloved hand. "After you and Noah helped us with that fence, it's the least we can do." A speeding driver had taken out a good portion of Jim's fence line along the highway a few months back, and Dad and Noah had helped him put up a temporary barrier.

As Jim and his son pulled away, Dad and Jude piled into the pickup and drove the remaining cattle to a smaller pasture. Once the cows were off-loaded, they headed back to the house for some lunch.

"It's been a while since we've discussed you taking over the cattle business." Dad eased the truck and empty trailer alongside the barn. "'Course things haven't been what I would call normal around here either."

"No, they haven't." Jude exited the vehicle and followed his father across the drive, up the steps of the deck and into the house. After pausing in the mudroom to remove their boots and hats—a rule his mother had drummed into all of their heads from the moment they were old enough to wear boots—they washed their hands before continuing through the living room and into the adjoining kitchen.

Dad swung open the door to the fridge. "Roast beef sandwich?"

"Sounds good to me." Jude grabbed a glass from the cupboard and filled it at the tap. He took a long swig, then moved to the pantry for a bag of potato chips.

"I assume you've been mulling over my offer." Knife in hand, the old man cut the roast into thin slices.

Maybe not the offer, per se. Simply how to tell the man no. He sucked in a breath. "I have."

Dad looked at him over his shoulder, a smile lifting one corner of his mouth. "And?"

"Well, it's like this."

His father's phone rang. He set the knife on the counter and pulled the device from his shirt pocket to look at the screen. "Hillary. I'd better take this." He tapped the screen and placed the phone to his ear. "Hello."

Jude opened the bag and grabbed a handful of chips. He was starving.

"No, you do not need to call a tow truck. At least, not yet."

That didn't sound good.

The old man continued to listen as he moved into the living room. "I know, but we're finished now." He again fell quiet. Then, "Don't you worry, darlin'." There was a tenderness in the old man's voice that Jude hadn't heard since his mother passed. "I'll be there quick as I can." He ended the call and shoved the phone back in his pocket.

"Problem?"

Dad was already on his way into the mudroom. "Hillary's car quit on her up near Colona. I'm gonna go see if I can figure out what's wrong."

Jude followed him. "Her vehicle isn't that old, is it?"

"Couple years. Let's just hope it's somethin' simple." He shoved his feet into his well-worn boots, donned his cowboy hat and headed for the door. "Don't know when I'll be back. If we have to tow it, it may be a while."

Jude wasn't sure if he should be relieved or disappointed. Just when he'd finally mustered up the courage... "No problem. You just do what you gotta do."

Saturday morning, Kayla stared into the smaller of two upstairs bedrooms inside of Livie's House. This was it. The start of her new life.

A plethora of emotions ricocheted through her, most of them good. She'd wanted a do-over. She just never imagined her life would change so dramatically. A new town, new job, new place to live... And, of course, a baby.

"This space would be perfect for a nursery." Lily paced the room, hands clasped against her chest, her excitement almost palpable. "All this natural light." She gestured to the two windows. "And this greige color—" smoothing a hand across one wall, she faced Kayla "—is the perfect backdrop for just about anything. No matter what color bedding and accents you choose, whether feminine or masculine, everything will look great."

Funny, this tour of her new abode with Lily was much different from the one Jude had given her last night. Then again, a tour was simply an excuse so they could be alone. He'd come by after work, disheartened that he hadn't been able to break the news to his father about the cattle business, after all. And since the recently renovated home used to belong to his grandmother...

Yet while Jude had given her a basic walk-through of the house, Lily shared ideas on how to make it a home.

"I'm not sure how I feel about having the baby's room upstairs while my bedroom is downstairs. What if I don't hear him or her?"

"That's what baby monitors are for. And they even have video monitors now, so you can actually see the baby." Lily crossed to stand beside Kayla. "Another option would be for you to take the other bedroom up here and use the bedroom downstairs for a guest room or office." She shrugged. "Only difference is that the bathroom up here is down the hall, whereas the one downstairs is adjoining."

"Good point." She crossed the hall to the other bedroom that boasted a queen-size bed and farmhouse-style furnishings. Leaning against the doorjamb, she contemplated the inviting space. The downstairs bedroom was decorated similarly, though it was slightly larger.

Taking a deep breath, she looked at her friend, who remained in the hallway. "What would you recommend?"

"Downstairs. At least for the time being. Baby isn't due for at least three months. And once it arrives, the doctor may not want you climbing stairs for a while. So, you may as well start down there where there's plenty of room for a bassinet."

Kayla couldn't help smiling. She hugged her friend. "I'm so glad you're back."

Releasing her, Lily said, "No offense, but I wouldn't have minded a few more days alone with my husband."

Suddenly craving another one of the cinnamon rolls Lily had brought from Granny's Kitchen, Kayla headed for the steps. "You mean you don't regret not jetting off to somewhere exotic?"

Lily followed. "Been there, done that. For now, I prefer to keep things simple. As long as I'm with Noah, any place is perfect."

At the bottom of the stairs, Kayla faced her friend. "Aww...look at you. All mushy with love."

Lily playfully swatted her. "Hey, you could find yourself here one day, too."

Kayla continued across the beautiful hardwood floors into the bright white kitchen. Though she'd been here once or twice all those years ago, she didn't recall things looking this good. If memory served her correctly, the kitchen had been mixture of gold countertops and green appliances.

"I doubt that." Using a fork, she lifted another roll from the foil pan on the peninsula. "Want one?"

"No, thanks." Lily eyed her from the other side of the peninsula. "And don't be such a doubting Thomas, because I said the same thing."

"Yes, you did." Setting the roll on her plate, Kayla lifted a shoulder. "Still…"

"Kayla, not every guy is like Shane."

"I know." Picking up her plate, she moved to the oval wooden table near the window. "But then I never suspected Shane was like Shane either."

Lily joined her. "Alcoholics are good at hiding things. You only see what they want you to see."

Kayla picked up the roll. "I suppose you're right. Even his parents never knew. You should have seen how shocked they were when the coroner told them his blood alcohol level was three times the legal limit." She took a bite of the gooey goodness. "By the way, I told Jude about Shane."

"That was brave of you."

She waited until she'd finished chewing

to respond. "I wanted—no, needed—him to know I'm different now."

"Why? Don't you think he could figure it out?"

"Maybe." She licked her fingers. "But I always get the feeling that he still thinks of me as that girl he once knew instead of who I am now."

"Perhaps he sees something that you don't. Something you only thought was gone."

"Perhaps." Though highly doubtful.

"I just want you to be open to whatever God might have in store for you. Not to mention that little one growing inside of you."

"Speaking of growing." Kayla stood. "Did you notice I'm wearing maternity clothes? Courtesy of Carly." She modeled the skinny jeans and striped shirt.

"That is so cute."

Kayla felt the baby kick. She laid a hand over the spot. "I think somebody else likes cinnamon rolls, too."

Lily's eyes grew wide. She jumped to

her feet. "The baby's moving?" She placed both hands on Kayla's belly.

"I felt it for the first time the night of the wedding. I went to the doctor this week, too, and he did a sonogram. The baby was sucking its thumb."

Anticipation lit Lily's face. Finally, the baby moved again.

"Oh…" she cooed. "That is so sweet. I can hardly wait to hold it."

This was the perfect time. "Lily?" She waited for her friend to look at her before she continued. "Would you be my birthing coach?"

"Oh, sweetie." She pooched out her bottom lip, then hugged her tight. "I would be honored."

Across the room, Kayla's cell phone rang. She freed herself and hurried to the counter, unplugged it from its charger and looked at the screen. The sight of her mother-in-law's name made her cringe.

Not only had she not talked to her in-laws since coming to Ouray, she now had to tell them that she planned to stay here.

"Sorry, Lily. It's my mother-in-law." She pressed the button and placed the phone to her ear. "Hi, Maureen."

"Hello, Kayla. I just wanted to check in with you, see how your trip went."

This was it. Time to tell them her plans had changed and then hope they'd be happy for her. After all, Joe and Maureen Bradshaw had always been kind to her. Sure, Joe was a little gruff and liked to control things, but he cared about his family. Which made it even more difficult to keep Shane's secret hidden from them. "Very well. Actually, I'm still in Ouray."

"Still? But you've been gone for two weeks."

"I know. However, I was presented with a job opportunity in Ouray that I just couldn't turn down."

"You...you mean you're staying in Ouray?" She heard the quiver in Maureen's voice.

"I was planning to call you tomorrow to let you know."

"But what about the baby?"

"I've already been to a doctor here who has agreed to take over my prenatal care."

"So, the baby will be born out there?" The disappointment in her mother-in-law's voice was killing her.

"Yes."

"But who will care for the child?"

Her eyes closed momentarily. How could she have forgotten? Though she had yet to give the woman an answer, Maureen had made it clear that she wanted to be the baby's caretaker as opposed to a day care.

"I...haven't figured that out yet." She rubbed her forehead. She'd definitely need to start looking into that soon.

"Kayla, are you sure you've thought this through?"

Kayla eyed the large spruce in the backyard. "Yes, ma'am." Though that didn't stop the second guesses from niggling at her now.

"All right. If you feel that would be best, then I guess there's nothing else to say."

"I'll send you my contact information—"

She looked at her phone to see the call had been disconnected.

On the other side of the peninsula, Lily bit her bottom lip. "How did she take it?"

"She was definitely disappointed." And Kayla knew the woman well enough to know that she was probably crying her eyes out right now. Something that only made her feel worse. And had her wondering if she'd truly done the right thing.

Chapter Twelve

Jude could hardly wait to show Kayla the crib designs he'd sketched for her. He had one that was definitively rustic, another with clean lines that could also convert into a toddler bed when the child got older and a final option, which was a little more elegant with a curved head and footboard. Now he was eager to see which one she would choose.

So, armed with a supreme pizza with extra cheese, he made his way up the walk just before six thirty Saturday evening to what had once been his grandmother's house. In her seemingly infinite wisdom, his mother's mother had willed half of the house to her friend and next-door neighbor, Carly, and the other half to his brother Andrew—a move that ended up reuniting the former high school sweethearts. Something Jude suspected his grandmother had been hoping for all along.

He rang the bell, anticipating Kayla had been far too busy unpacking and getting settled to even think about eating. After all, moving could be a monumental task. Given what had happened at the wedding, he wasn't about to take any risks.

A few moments later, the door opened.

"Jude." Wearing a long, bulky cardigan over a striped shirt and her hair pulled back in a ponytail, Kayla looked almost bewildered, tentative, and seemed to cling to the door like a lifeline. "What are you doing here?"

Perhaps he should have called first. "I brought you some dinner." He held out the large pizza.

"Oh." She stared at the box before lifting her wide-eyed gaze to his. "Um…come on in." She held the door open, motioning for him to enter.

Hmm. Not exactly the reaction he'd expected. Yet as he moved into what his grandmother had always referred to as the parlor, he caught the scent of something spicy and sweet. Had someone else already brought her dinner? Carly, maybe, since she lived next door and cooked all the time anyway.

"Smells like somebody already brought you some food."

"No." She pushed the door closed, worry lines creasing her brow when she looked at him. "*I've* been cooking."

"You?" He'd never known her to cook before. Then again, they'd both been living with their parents. Since then she'd been married, had a home of her own... "I thought you'd be busy unpacking."

"It's a furnished house." She waved a hand, bringing attention to the nicely appointed living room. "All I had to unpack were my clothes and some personal items."

"Ah. Good point." One he'd obviously overlooked.

"Besides, I like to cook. Especially when I'm stressed."

Concern arched his brow. "What are you stressed about?"

Her mouth opened as though she was going to say something, then snapped shut as she turned and moved into the kitchen.

He followed her with the pizza. "Kayla, what are you stressed about?"

Inside the recently updated kitchen, she lifted the lid on what appeared to be a pot of chili and gave it a stir. "I'm not stressed. I simply meant that cooking is good therapy when I am."

"Uh-huh." He eyed the dozens of cookies spread across the counter and peninsula and wondered what army she was planning to feed. "Looks like you don't need this pizza then."

"Are you kidding?" She hastily replaced the lid, dropped the spoon and took the box from him. "There's never a bad time for pizza." She set it beside her laptop on the table and grabbed a slice. "Can I interest you in a bowl of chili?"

"Depends. What kind of cookies are those?"

She glanced at the counter. "Oatmeal raisin, peanut butter and chocolate chip."

"That's a lot of cookies."

Her shoulder lifted. "I couldn't decide which one I was hungry for so I made them all."

He studied her for a moment. The worry lines he'd noticed when he first came in hadn't been there yesterday and they had yet to dissipate. "In that case, I'll take a peanut butter cookie, *then* the chili."

While she ladled up the chili, he grabbed a cookie, nibbling on it as he took in the image on her computer screen. "What's this?"

Peering over her shoulder, she said, "At the moment, it's a work in progress." She retrieved a spoon from the drawer, added it to the bowl and continued toward him. "But eventually it will be a 3-D design of the new and improved Congress Hotel."

"Is this like one of those CAD programs?"

"That's exactly what it is." She handed him the bowl. "I took some classes several years ago, figuring it would help whenever I presented designs to my boss. Now it'll give me the drawings I'll need when I submit my application for permits on the hotel."

"This is amazing." Bowl in one hand, spoon in the other, he was about to take a bite when his gaze drifted to the professional-looking sketches beside the computer. "Did you draw these?"

"Yeah." She reached for the one on top. "I'm trying to come up with the best layout for the guest rooms. Since there was no indoor plumbing when the hotel was built, the bathrooms that were added later aren't connected to any of the rooms."

"And who wants to go down the hall to use the restroom in a hotel?"

"Exactly. Now each room will have a private bath, I just need to determine the most cost-effective way to configure everything without it feeling like an afterthought."

He thought about the crib sketches tucked in his back pocket. While they were good, they were crude compared to what Kayla had done.

Facing her, he saw the skepticism in her expression and wondered if she had any idea just how much talent she possessed. "Kayla, this is amazing. Not only would most general contractors pay somebody to do this—" he nodded toward the computer "—but you have a real gift. You can see beyond what exists and envision what could be."

Appearing suddenly nervous, she closed the lid on the laptop. "I've still got a long way to go. I just hope I can get it right."

Why was she doubting herself? "Well, based on what I just saw, not only will you get it right, you'll knock it out of the ballpark."

The corners of her mouth twitched. "I appreciate the encouragement."

Man, that husband of hers had really done a number on her. Stripping her of her confidence. Something Jude was determined to rectify.

"I'm just speaking the truth." He took a bite of chili before setting his bowl on the table. "Now I have something to show you." Pulling the sketches from his pocket, he closed the lid on the pizza box, giving him space to spread them out. "I'd like to make a crib for your baby." He laid out each design. "Though they're pretty rough, I've got some sketches here I'd like you to look at so I'll know which style you prefer."

When she didn't say anything, he looked up to discover her still at the end of the table.

"You kind of need to come here so you can see them," he said.

Ever so slightly, she shook her head. "I'm sorry, I can't."

"Why not?"

"Because I can't let you do that."

"Make you a crib? Why not?"

"Because it's too much." She looked

at her clasped hands. "And I don't even know if—"

He moved toward her again. "Don't know if what?"

She turned away, but he moved in front of her.

"Talk to me, Kayla. What's going on? You've been acting strange the entire time I've been here."

With a sigh, she dropped into one of the six wooden chairs. "My mother-in-law called today, assuming I was back in Denver. When I told her I was staying in Ouray, she was really disappointed."

Taking a seat in the adjacent chair, he leaned toward her, resting his forearms on his thighs. "I don't mean to sound insensitive, but that's her problem, not yours. You have to do what's right for you."

"I know. And I thought I was doing the right thing. I mean, just look at how everything has fallen into place for me to stay in Ouray."

"Yes, it has."

"But…"

Unfortunately, he knew exactly where this was leading. "After talking to her, you're second-guessing your decision?"

Lowering her pretty head, Kayla nodded. She was allowing herself to be manipulated again, like she had with her husband.

He reached for her hands. "Kayla, nobody can decide what's right for you but you. Sure, others might be disappointed, but this is your life. What do you want?"

"For everybody to be happy."

"Yeah, well, that's never going to happen." That earned him a smile. He squeezed her hands. "Let me ask you this. When you informed your mother that you were going to stay in Denver, what did she say?"

"Initially, she tried to talk me out of it. Until she realized how determined I was. Then she hugged me and told me she wanted me to be happy." Kayla straightened then, looking as though she'd just had a lightbulb moment. "I never would have dreamed I'd have an opportunity to work on something the scale of the Congress Hotel." She looked at him, determination lighting her chestnut eyes. "I really want to prove to myself, and the world, that I can do it."

He couldn't help but grin. "Then do it. Trust your instincts."

She gave a soft laugh. "Thank you. It's been so long since someone asked me what I wanted that I forget to ask myself."

"Glad I could help. Now—" he shoved to his feet "—if you'll allow me, I'd really like to show you these crib designs."

Her smile faltered then. "Why?"

"Because your baby needs a place to sleep." He peered down at her. "And since I've never made a crib before, I thought it'd be fun. Humor me."

She grinned in force then, and he thought his heart might beat right out of his chest. "In that case, let's see what you've got."

Jude was right. It was time for Kayla to focus on what she wanted and stop trying to make everyone else happy. However, if it made him happy to make her baby a crib, then that was fine by her.

All three of the designs he'd shown her two nights ago far exceeded the basic crib she'd been planning to purchase, and narrowing it down to just one had been tough. In the end, though, she'd decided to go with the one with the arched head and foot because it would showcase Jude's woodworking skills. After all, a gift from him should display his talent.

Now if she could just nail down the layout for the third-floor guest rooms.

"Lily threw me a bit of a curveball when she stopped by earlier today." Standing in the narrow hallway of the hotel's upper level, she eyed Jude. "She'd like to have a suite. Complete with a king-size bed, clawfoot tub with a separate shower and a sitting area."

"Where did she propose you put this suite?" Still wearing his police shirt, cargo pants and tactical belt, Jude glanced from one end of the hall to the other.

"She's leaving that part up to me."

"Okay—" the corners of his mouth

twitched "—so where are *you* going to put it?"

"That's why I asked you to come by." Moving to the western end of the hall, she opened the doors to the rooms on either side. "The only solution I've been able to come up with is to combine the space of these two rooms into one room that runs from the front of the hotel to the back." She walked into the small room that sat at the front of the hotel, the last remnants of late-afternoon sunlight struggling to make it through the southern-and western-facing windows.

"We could have the sitting area here, in front of the windows so guests could enjoy this spectacular view of Mount Hayden. Then—" she retraced her steps back to the door "—the bed would be somewhere in here." She gestured with her arms. "Probably a dresser opposite. And the other room—" she pointed "—would be where the bathroom is located."

"Entrance?"

"Either here—" she noted a spot on the

bedroom wall "—or into the short hallway connecting the bedroom and bathroom. Which is also where the closet would be."

Jude walked between the two tiny rooms, nodding. "I think it's perfect."

She followed him into the room across the hall. "Don't be silly. Nothing is perfect."

Hands perched low on his hips, he frowned at her. "Look, a suite is an upgraded room. Usually with more space, a nice place to sit... You've achieved that *and* given guests an incredible view to boot. In my book, that's perfect."

She pondered his words, still uncertain. "I know, but..."

"But what?"

An image of the finished room played across her mind, the way it had earlier in the day after her meeting with Lily. She could envision guests sitting in cozy chairs that faced the window and that glorious view. And the bathroom with its classic black-and-white mosaic floor, marble walk-in shower and luxurious claw-foot tub… Guests might never want to leave.

"Nothing." She met Jude's dark gaze. "I agree. It is perfect."

"Are you saying I'm right?"

"No. I'm saying I am."

He laughed. "It's about time you realized that."

Thanks to him. This wasn't the first time he'd forced her to take a good, hard look at herself or her ideas. Much the way her father used to. Only one of many reasons she adored her dad. Hugh Brennan had always believed in her.

She surreptitiously watched the man beside her. Jude believed in her, too.

The realization sent an unexpected wave of awareness shivering through her. But she quickly shook it off. Jude was her friend. And she was pregnant with another man's child. Meaning any and all romantic notions were off-limits. For the sake of her baby, she couldn't afford to make another mistake.

"You about ready to call it a day?" Jude's question interrupted her reverie.

"Yeah, I think so."

"Good." He followed as she started for the stairs. "Don't suppose I could talk you into a hot drink from Mouse's and stroll around town, could I?"

After spending all day in the stale hotel, she could use a dose of fresh air. "I like the way you think, Officer Stephens."

In the lobby, she grabbed her coat and draped it over her arm.

"You'll probably want to put that on." He took the coat and held it up for her. "It's kind of cool out there today."

"Another front come through?" She shoved her arms into the sleeves.

"Yep." He moved toward the door. "Winter will be here before we know it."

Ten minutes later, their fingers were wrapped around lidded cups of hot apple cider.

Kayla took a sip. "Mmm... I'm so glad you suggested this. Very autumnal."

"What can I say?" Steam billowed from

the tiny hole in the lid of his cup as they walked up Main Street. "I'm an *autumnal* kind of guy."

"Whatever." She rolled her eyes. "So where would you like to go?"

"There's a recently renovated house over off Fourth." At the corner, he reached for her elbow and kept his hand there as they started across the street. "I thought you might like to see it." His caring touch made it difficult to concentrate.

"Yeah, sure."

"How's the overall layout of the hotel coming? Aside from Lily's curveball, that is."

"Pretty good. I think I'm finally starting to get a good feel for everything. I may try to work on adding the suite into the computer tonight."

"Sounds like you're truckin' right along."

"Time is money." A breeze sifted through a large blue spruce as she followed him around a corner. "The sooner I get the permits, the sooner we can start demoing. I want to get as much done as possible before the baby comes."

"I know you do."

Looking up, she spotted her favorite house, in all of its mustard-yellow-and-raspberry ugliness. Then she saw the for-sale sign in the front yard. Funny, that wasn't there two weeks ago.

Her steps slowed as they approached the house, images of her mental renovations plaguing her mind and accelerating her heart rate. This was the opportunity she'd always hoped for.

"Something wrong?" Concern marred Jude's handsome features as he watched her curiously.

"No, not at all. Actually, something's very right."

"Care to share?"

She pointed to the Realtor's sign. "It's for sale."

He grinned then. "You always did love this house."

"I still do." She looked from Jude to the

house and back. "How much do you think they're asking?"

"Hard to say. It's historic, but it's also in pretty bad shape. You might not be able to move in right away. Not until you've made sure it's safe for the baby."

"Remember that room with all the windows?"

"We agreed it would make a great kids' room." The fact that he remembered had her already-flailing emotions behaving like a hyperactive child jazzed on sugar.

"Yeah." She stared at the house, trying to bring her crazy thoughts under control. Something that wasn't easy with Jude watching her. But, boy, would she love to have this house. "I wonder if there are any major issues with the place. You know, the kind that translate to big bucks."

"Well, that porch will need to be shored up pretty quickly. That shouldn't be too expensive, though. However—" setting a hand on her shoulder, he turned her to face him "—first things first. Call the Realtor, find out what they're asking, then make an appointment to look at it. You never know, things could be so bad you don't even want to consider it."

She simply blinked. That would be like breaking up with a longtime love. "You're right. This could be way out of my price range."

"And if it isn't?"

Then her dream had come true. She eyed the man beside her. One of them anyway.

Chapter Thirteen

Jude was falling in love with Kayla all over again.

Not that he'd ever stopped loving her. But the feelings that accompanied it—the heart-pounding anticipation of spending time with her, the thrill of seeing her name appear on his phone—had him turned inside out. Just the way they had seven years ago.

Every once in a while, he'd catch glimpses of the old Kayla. Her confidence was returning. And the look on her face when she saw that the old Orr house was on the market... If he wasn't a goner already, he was then. Once upon a time, he'd dreamed of sharing that house with her. Him, Kayla and a whole passel of kids.

Did he dare to dream again? Or was he setting himself up for another heartache?

He wasn't sure he had the answer to either of those questions. All he knew was that he couldn't wait to see her tonight.

So, while she went to look at the house this Saturday morning, he had work to do. Over the past week, he'd spent so much time with Kayla that he'd gotten behind on his orders. And if he didn't get caught up, he could kiss his plans for the real date he'd scheduled at a nice restaurant tonight goodbye.

A blast of cold air filtered into the shop just then. In the past few days, temperatures had taken a drastic tumble. He could only pray that any snow would hold off until after tonight.

"Jude."

He hated the way he cringed every time he heard his father call his name. It didn't used to be that way. He used to greet the old man with a smile and ask him how his day was going. Yet in the weeks since the topic of taking over the cattle business had been broached, things had changed.

Jude should have given him his answer a long time ago. That first night, even. But instead of ripping off the bandage with one quick yank, he'd been slowly peeling it back, causing himself even more pain in the long run.

The man paused just inside the door, his expression stern. "I need to see you inside. Your brothers are all here, and I think it's time we had a talk."

Before Jude could respond, his father was gone, leaving a bone-chilling dread in his wake.

A knot the size of Mount Sneffels twisted in his gut. This was it. With everyone here, Dad was probably going to announce that Jude was taking over the cattle business. How would he get out of this now? He'd either have to tell the man no and embarrass the both of them in front of his brothers or give up his own business, the one *he'd* worked hard to build, and take care of the ranch until his father passed away.

Whichever path he chose, someone was going to get hurt. All because he wasn't man enough to come clean with his father before.

Grabbing his jacket, he mentally kicked himself all the way to the house. Now he wished he'd gone with Kayla, no matter how many orders he had.

The aroma of coffee and cinnamon rolls greeted him when he walked inside. Something he would have found tempting any other time. Now, however, he didn't have the stomach for either one.

After kicking off his boots in the mudroom, he made his way into the living room, where he spotted every other male in his family sitting around the table in the adjoining kitchen.

Cup of coffee in hand, Dad looked up. "Good, you're here. Have a seat." Smiling, he motioned to one of two empty chairs, the other having belonged to Jude's mother.

Jude's stomach tightened as he approached. "Dad, I—"

"I know, you've got orders to tend to. But this won't take long, so sit down."

Dropping into the wooden chair, he felt as though he was ten years old again. Somehow, he'd have to find a way to break the news to his father. Today.

Dad pushed his mug aside and clasped his hands together. "I asked you boys here today because I have something to tell you."

Jude swallowed hard.

"And I'd also like to hear your feedback."

Jude's head jerked up. Feedback? He hadn't anticipated that. This could be his chance for a reprieve. What if one of his brothers balked? What if they wanted the cattle business?

"Dad—" creases formed on Noah's brow and around his eyes "—the last time you gathered all of us around like this it was to tell us Mama had cancer. You're not sick, are you?"

The old man's eyes widened in surprise. "No. No. Sorry, boys."

The collective release of breath around the table was almost audible.

"I didn't mean to worry you, but I do have something important to discuss with you."

Okay, now it was a discussion. Jude could handle that. Except, now Dad looked nervous.

"I..." He met each of their gazes. "I'm going to propose to Hillary, and I want to know if any of you have any objections."

Jude and his brothers looked at one another, each of them wearing the same dumbfounded expression. Dad was asking their permission to get married?

"Well, that was unexpected." His youngest brother Daniel slouched in his chair.

"No, it wasn't," said Andrew. "Our wives—" he pointed from himself to Matt and Noah "—have been expecting this for a while now."

"They have?" Seemed it was Dad's turn to look surprised.

Matt patted him on the shoulder. "It's okay, Dad. We know you can be a little slow on the uptake."

The old man glared at his middle son.

"Actually, this is happening a little quicker than I'd expected." Noah eyed their father. "Though, I was expecting it." His big brother grinned. "Have you bought the ring yet?"

Dad reached into his pocket and pulled out a velvet box, his hands shaking.

He lifted the lid to reveal a ring with a decent-sized center diamond encircled by a series of smaller diamonds.

Andrew let go a low whistle. "What are you trying to do, make us look bad?" Again he motioned between himself, Matt and Noah.

"I hope she likes it." Dad closed the box and wrapped his hand around it.

"She will, Dad." Noah assured with a smile.

"Does this mean you boys are good with my decision?"

The five of them looked at each other.

"I'm good." Noah raised his hand the same way they'd done when they were kids taking a family vote.

"Me, too." Andrew raised his hand.

"Ditto," said Matt.

"I'm good," Jude added.

All eyes were on their baby brother now. While the rest of them had been around to watch Dad and Hillary's relationship develop, Daniel, the adventurer in the family, had been gone a lot, traveling the world, and hadn't had the chance to get to know Hillary until this past summer.

The only Stephens boy who favored their mother with her blond hair and blue eyes looked at the old man across the table. "You and Mama had a lot of good years together. I know you miss her just as much as we do. But I also know that she'd want you to be happy." His gaze bounced to each of his brothers. "So, I'm good, too."

Applause erupted as everyone congratulated their father. Jude felt a giant sense of relief, albeit only temporary. He still had to come clean with his dad.

Yet as he watched the old man now, something else crossed Jude's mind. What if Dad wanted to retire so he could be with Hillary? And if he did, could Jude bring himself to deny him that?

Was this a real date?

Kayla stared at her reflection in the full-length mirror early that evening. Perhaps the sweater dress and boots were too much. Jude had only asked her to dinner, after all. In Montrose. Just the two of them.

She blew out a breath and dropped onto the side of the quilt-covered bed. It couldn't be a date. Pregnant women didn't date. Did they?

What had she been thinking?

You weren't thinking. You were too busy getting lost in those dark eyes of his.

Truth be known, she liked spending time with Jude. He made her feel normal again. The way he encouraged her, believed in her, made her feel as though she could do anything she set her mind to. And she couldn't wait to tell him about the house.

A knock sounded at the door.

Her gaze shot to the clock on the nightstand. Jude wasn't supposed to be here for another thirty minutes.

Standing, she started for the door. She didn't know who else it could be, so if it was him, he'd just have to wait.

She flipped on the porch light and peered through the peephole. Unease swept through her veins. What were Shane's parents, Joe and Maureen Bradshaw, doing here?

Her insides twisted as she recalled her phone conversation with Maureen last week.

When she sent them her address, she never imagined they'd show up in Ouray. Maybe when the baby came, but not now.

A louder knock made her jump. Joe wasn't known for his patience.

She drew in a deep breath and opened the door. "Joe? Maureen?" Her gaze darted between the two. "What a surprise." Not necessarily a good one either. "What are you doing here?"

"We came to see you, young lady." Joe scowled. "The least you could do is let us in." While she'd grown accustomed to her father-in-law's gruffness, she certainly hadn't missed it.

"Of course." She held the door wide, hoping they weren't planning to stay with her. Denver was five hours away, and it was already dark. Fortunately, Ouray had plenty of hotels.

The petite woman with short brown hair dutifully followed her husband, clutching the collar of her coat. Once they were inside, Kayla noticed her mother-in-law's red-rimmed eyes.

"Please, have a seat." She gestured toward the plush gray sofa against the wall.

"That won't be necessary." Hands shoved in the pockets of his loose-fitting work pants, Joe continued to frown. "We're not here to chitchat."

Apprehension snaked up Kayla's spine as she shifted from one booted foot to the other. "What...can I help you with?"

"Young lady, why are you doing this to us?"

"What am I doing?"

"This whole nonsense about moving to Ouray. It's ridiculous. You don't know a soul out here, except for that socialite who got married. Do you have any idea how difficult this has been for Maureen?"

Seeing the woman's bottom lip tremble tore at Kayla's heart. She never wanted to hurt them.

"She's been looking forward to this baby for months," Joe continued. "Now she's losing it just like we lost Shane."

Kayla straightened, her hand automatically covering her belly. "That's not true. I would never try to keep this baby away from you. It is now and will always be your grandchild. But please understand that I have to think about what's best for my baby. I've been offered a wonderful job opportunity here." She lifted a shoulder. "Besides… I really need a fresh start."

"Why?" No-nonsense Joe looked at her like she was crazy. "I mean, sure you're heartbroken about Shane. We all are. But you can't raise a baby alone."

She could, and she would. Just like she would have if Shane were still alive. Unfortunately, Shane's parents had never known about his drinking. How could she make them understand now?

"Shane and I had...problems in our marriage."

"Every marriage has problems, dear." A timid Maureen practically squeaked out the words.

"Yes, I—I understand that." Except the issues between her and Shane went far beyond the average disagreement. "But..." *You have to tell them.* She wrapped her arms around her midsection. "You know how the authorities said that Shane's blood alcohol level was three times the legal limit?"

Joe grumbled. "I still don't understand that. Shane never drank."

"Not in front of you, he didn't."

Joe and Maureen looked at each other curiously.

"What are you saying?" Her father-in-law's intimidating dark gaze narrowed on Kayla.

She drew in a bolstering breath. *God, I don't want to hurt them. Please help them to see the truth.* "Shane was an alcoholic."

Maureen gasped, her hand covering her mouth as tears filled her blue eyes.

"That's a lie." Joe spewed the words, his face turning redder by the second. "How dare you speak ill of my son. Shane was a fine Christian man."

"He tried to be, yes." Her voice quivered. "But he had a problem."

"That's enough." The vehemence spilling from Joe had her taking a step back. "If Shane drank at all, it was probably because you drove him to it. Well, we will not stand here and let you slander our son." Joe took hold of a sobbing Maureen's arm, practically dragging her toward the door.

Kayla followed them, her own tears stinging the backs of her eyes. "I'm not trying to slander him. I'm simply trying to explain why I need to leave Denver." *God, please make them understand.*

Still on the porch, Joe glared back at her. "You've taken everything that Shane worked so hard to achieve. His house, his money, now you want to keep his child from us. And, so help me God—" he ground out the words "—I will *not* let that happen."

The storm door slapped closed with Maureen's sobs still echoing in Kayla's ears.

She shut the door, collapsing against it, regretting the fact that she'd never said anything to them before. If she had, maybe Shane could have gotten the help he so desperately needed. That is, if they'd believed her.

Wrapping her arms around herself again, she dropped onto the sofa and allowed her tears to fall. *God, why is this so hard? I want to be here, but did I misunderstand Your will for my life? Am I supposed to go back to Denver?*

She was still on the couch when someone knocked on the door again.

Jude. Oh, no. She'd forgotten about their date. But she sure could stand to see a friendly face. Why was it he always seemed to show up when she needed him most?

Standing, she tried to swipe away her tears, likely smearing her mascara in the process. If there was any left.

He knocked again. "Kayla?"

"Coming." She sniffed and moved to open the door. "I'm not quite ready," she said as he walked in wearing a pair of dark chinos and a button-down shirt.

"I'll say." Brow puckered with concern, he stared at her. "What's wrong?"

That was all it took. One look into his compassion-filled gaze, and the tears fell anew.

"Aw, Kayla." His muscular arms enveloped her as he pressed her head against his chest. "It's okay. I'm here. Shh…" He stroked her hair and her back, but most of all, he held her close to his heart, in the safe haven of his embrace. Something she wasn't even aware she needed until now.

He held her until she stopped crying, not asking any questions. Knowing they were inevitable, though, she reluctantly lifted her head and peered up at him. "Shane's parents were here."

"When?" He loosened his hold but didn't let her go.

"Shortly before you arrived."

"What did they want?"

Suddenly needing space, she stepped away to pace the beige-and-gray area rug as she told him all that had transpired. Including telling the Bradshaws their son was an alcoholic.

"Uh-oh."

"Yeah." Her shoulders sagged. "They accused me of lying. Said—" her voice cracked "—I was trying to slander their son."

Jude's nostrils flared. "They sure don't know you very well, do they?"

"Maybe not. But I can't help thinking,

perhaps, I should just go back to Denver so everyone will be happy."

"Not everyone." He closed what little space was between them. "Would returning to Denver make you happy?"

She didn't even have to think. "No. It feels good to be in Ouray again. Like it's where I belong."

"That's what I thought." He rubbed her upper arms. "Because you're getting the do-over you wanted. Don't them guilt you into giving that up."

Looking up at him, she smiled. "You're right. This is *my* life, and I can do whatever *I* want."

His grin grew wide. "That's my girl."

Strange, not long ago she would have balked at being called his girl. Right now, though, it sounded kind of nice.

"By the way, did you see the house?"

"I did." With the Bradshaws' drama, she'd almost forgotten. But she smiled in earnest.

"And…?"

"It has promise."

"Good. Why don't you tell me all about it over dinner then?" He never took his eyes off her. He just kept looking at her as though she was the most important person in the world. "We can order in or go out. The choice is up to you."

She really was looking forward to a nice dinner. And since she was already dressed… "Let's go out. Just give me five minutes to fix my face."

"Why?" He caressed her cheek with the back of his hand, sending a wave of chill bumps down her arms that had nothing to do with the weather. "I think you look beautiful just the way you are."

Chapter Fourteen

Kayla pulled up to the ranch house early the next afternoon. At church this morning, both Lily and Jude had assured her this was one family meal she wouldn't want to miss. She wasn't sure what that meant, but she'd be happy to settle for a relaxing afternoon free of any drama.

Shifting her truck into Park, she thought about her date with Jude last night. Despite everything that had transpired with the Bradshaws earlier in the evening, dinner had been delightful. The restaurant was much nicer than she'd expected. Kind of rustic, yet intimate. But what she remembered most was Jude telling her she was beautiful.

It had been a long time since anyone had complimented her like that. Even when Shane did, it was usually nothing more than an attempt to help right another wrong. But with Jude, she hadn't discounted his sincerity, even though she probably looked a mess when he'd said it.

Unlike her late husband, Jude didn't say or do anything strictly for face value. With him, things always had heart value. And that terrified her. She'd fallen in love twice in her life and both times had ended in heartbreak. She didn't want to go through that ever again. Especially now. Things were no longer just about her. She had a child to consider.

Gray skies hinted at snow, and the temperature was downright bone-chilling as she set her fur-lined boots onto the gravel. Fortunately, judging by the empty deck, it didn't appear they'd be eating outside.

She hugged her wool coat around her, realizing it barely covered her belly. Looked like she'd need to find herself another to see her through the delivery. In these temps, her baby could freeze while still in the womb.

Jude opened the door before she even made it onto the deck, as though he'd been watching for her. His smile said he was glad to see her.

"Come on in before you freeze." He held the door wide as she passed. "Looks like Hillary and her family are finally here, too." He nodded toward the drive.

Kayla looked out the window to see two SUVs bumping up the road. "How many people are we talking about?"

"Five. Her daughter, Celeste, and Celeste's husband, Gage, along with their three kids."

She peered up at him. "Looks like you're going to have quite a crowd."

"It's definitely a party." He helped her with her coat, then placed a hand against the small of her back as he urged her into the living room and across the wood-look floor to the large oriental rug. "They're here," he announced as they entered.

"Oh, good." Standing near the opening to the kitchen, holding baby Lucas, Carly eyed her husband, who stood behind her, seemingly happy about Jude's statement.

"How do I look?" Wearing a gray plaid Western shirt with pearl snaps and dark-wash jeans with a sharp crease, Clint stood in front of Lily near the large picture window, his salt-and-pepper hair neatly combed.

"Like the handsome cowboy you are." Smiling, Lily adjusted his collar. "You'll do just fine."

"I hope you're right." The older man fidgeted.

Funny, Kayla had always considered Clint to be a very confident man. But something sure had him rattled today.

Jude escorted her to the overstuffed sofa where she joined Matt and his wife, Lacie, while Jude perched on the arm beside her. On the love seat opposite them,

Lily's son, Colton, and Carly's daughter, Megan, stared at handheld devices.

Adjusting the throw pillow behind her, Kayla scanned the medium-sized room, savoring the warmth from the wood-burning stove in the corner. Seemed everyone was here. All five brothers, wives, kids… Then she recalled what Jude and Lily had said earlier.

Yep, there was definitely something extra special about this family gathering, making her wonder why they'd invited her. She was glad they had, though. The Stephens family had always made her feel welcome. She'd just have to wait to find out what was going on.

The noise level in the house grew as Hillary's family made their way inside. The chatter of little girls increased as her two granddaughters sought out Jude's youngest nieces, Piper and Kenzie. Meanwhile, the adults exchanged warm greetings. And the aromas that filled the air had her stomach growling like a bear that'd just come out of hibernation.

After a moment, a stylishly dressed Hillary glanced suspiciously around the room. "Why is everyone in here instead of the kitchen?" Her gaze shifted to the television's darkened screen. "What? No football game?" Eyeing Clint across the room, she perched a hand on her hip. "And why are you so dressed up?"

He inched toward her then, a nervous smile pulling at the corners of his mouth. "Woman, you sure ask a lot of questions."

"If a situation calls for it, yes."

"Well then, I reckon it's my turn to do the askin' for a change." Stopping in front of her, he eased down on one knee.

Hillary's eyes widened. "What are you doing?"

"If I can get word in edgewise, I thought I might ask you to marry me." With that, he held up a velvet box and lifted the lid. "I love you, Hillary. And I'd like you to be my wife."

"I—" the pretty blonde blinked repeatedly "—I don't know what to say."

"Yes, might be a good response." Clint

continued to watch her. "What do you say, Hillary? Will you marry me?"

She pressed a hand to her chest. "I never— I mean, I just—" The hand moved to cover her mouth, her dark eyes shimmering with unshed tears.

"Clint, you've gone and done it now," said Celeste. "Nobody's ever seen my mother speechless before."

Everyone chuckled.

"One word, darlin'." Clint winked up at the woman he hoped to share his life with. "That's all I need to hear."

Her smile grew then, her head nodding. "Yes."

Cheers erupted as Clint stood, placed the ring on her finger and then cupped the face of his intended and kissed her.

The lump in Kayla's throat felt as big as a boulder. Love was a powerful emotion. One that had to be backed up by a commitment that would last. She could take heart in knowing she'd done that. Even if Shane hadn't.

Dinner had suddenly turned into a party,

just as Jude had said. The promise of love was something to celebrate, indeed.

When the meal was over, the kitchen was clean and folks were relaxing or had gone home, Jude whisked Kayla to his shop to show her the arches he'd made for the head and foot of her baby's crib.

"What do you think?" He held up one end of the crib's frame, along with one of the slats.

Staring at the intricately carved pieces, she was blown away by his talent. Seemed Jude had a knack for exceeding her expectations.

"I think you are a gifted artist." She closed the distance between them. Smoothed a hand over the wood. "And I also believe that my baby is going to have one of the coolest cribs I've ever seen."

"As it should." He stared down at her with an intensity she hadn't seen before. At least not lately. Setting the wood aside, he slid his arms around her waist—what was left of it anyway—and pulled her to him. His dark eyes seemed riveted to hers.

Any other time, the move would have made her nervous. But for some reason, being in the circle of his embrace felt right.

She rested a hand against his chest, feeling the taut muscles beneath his shirt. The aroma of coffee, cinnamon and sawdust emanated from him. A combination she found hard to resist. And she didn't.

When he lowered his head and touched his lips to hers, time faded away. In that moment, she felt as though she'd been freed from the chains of the distorted love that had held her captive in recent years. But this...this was real. Simple and pure. Making her wish she'd stayed in Ouray all those years ago.

When he pulled away, his breathing was ragged. He visually traced her face. Smiled. "Sorry, I guess I got caught up in the emotion of the day."

Emotion of the day? Seriously? He hadn't felt that magnetic pull between them? The sparks that flickered in the air around them when he held her?

The euphoric state she'd foolishly allowed herself to fall into evaporated. Of course, he hadn't felt it. It was all in her imagination. Even worse, he was right. Clint's proposal was romantic. Even she'd been sucked in, believing someone could love her again. Namely Jude.

They were friends. And coworkers. But that's all it would ever be.

And like it or not, she'd just have to learn to accept it.

Jude had dreamed of kissing Kayla again for almost seven years. Finally, his dream had come true. Boy, was it worth waiting for. She still fit perfectly in his arms. And her lips, so soft and sweet. Things had changed between them this past week. Making him wonder if a future with Kayla really was within the realm of possibility.

But when their kiss ended, she left, claiming there was something important she'd forgotten to do. That was Sunday. Now it was Wednesday, and he'd barely talked to her. Seemed she was busy whenever he called, giving him the distinct impression that she was trying to brush him off. Question was, why?

The chemistry between them was undeniable. That kiss had been comprised of two very willing participants.

Could that have been the problem? That she *was* willing and somehow felt bad about it?

After seeing her truck outside of the hotel, he decided to quit analyzing and made a run to the deli around the corner. He picked up her favorite sandwich, as well as one of his own, before heading back to surprise her.

"Lunchtime," he said as he pushed the door open.

Standing beside the long folding table that had been set up in the hotel's lobby to serve as a desk, workbench and lunch counter, Kayla jerked her gaze to his. Hands tucked in the pockets of her overalls, she opened her mouth, likely to object, but he cut her off.

"One Reuben on rye with extra sauce." He crossed the lobby and handed her the bag.

She looked from it to him, one brow lifted. "How did you know I was craving a Reuben?"

He lifted a shoulder. "I didn't. I just know how much you like them." He pointed to the brown paper sack. "There are also some chips and a roast beef sandwich for me. Hope you don't mind if I join you?"

"Aren't you on duty?"

"Yes, but I do get to eat lunch. I have my radio, and we're right in the heart of town."

She eyed the table. "Let me clear us a space." Resignation laced her voice.

He chose to ignore it. "Still working on the drawings?" He scooted a stack of papers out of the way.

"Yeah. I'm hoping to have everything done by Friday. That way I can turn in the application for permits next week."

"That's great." He pulled up a second metal folding chair and emptied the contents of the bag onto the table. "You, uh, haven't heard any more from your in-laws, have you?"

"No, thank God." Grabbing her sandwich, she eased into the chair opposite him. "Hopefully they got the hint."

"For sure." It still irked him that they'd ganged up on her like that, trying to coerce her into doing what they wanted without considering her feelings. Granted, they were hurting, but the fact that they wouldn't believe her when she told them about their son really bothered Jude. He could understand disappointment or even disbelief as they tried to absorb the truth, but to call her a liar?

Boy, if he'd been there...

"Anything new on the house front?" He opened his bag of chips, grabbed one and popped it in his mouth. Over dinner Saturday night, Kayla had filled him in on just about every aspect of the dilapidated Victorian. How it looked now compared to when they'd looked at it seven years ago. What issues would need to be taken care of right away versus those that could wait. He'd drunk in the excitement that had flickered in her eyes as she verbally walked him through the house. And then the way they deconstructed and re-constructed the place right there at the dinner table... It reminded him of old times.

"In thought, yes. In action, no."

"Guess that means you're still thinking about it?"

"I'm this close—" she held up her fore-finger and thumb with the slightest space in between "—to making a decision."

"Mind if I ask what that decision might be?"

She shrugged. "You can ask. Doesn't mean I have to answer." Her face was void of any expression.

He shifted in his seat. "Okay, did I do something wrong? Because I'm getting the feeling you just flung a dagger in my direction."

Leaning back in her chair, hands atop her growing stomach, she studied him. "Why are you here, Jude?"

He wasn't sure what was going on, but— "Because I wanted to see you. Surprise you with lunch. Ever since that kiss, you've been avoiding me. Why?"

She stared at her hands then. "I haven't been avoiding you." Looking up, she continued, "I just—" Lines creased her brow as her gaze drifted toward the door. "Joe." She stood. "Maureen." Crossing the wooden floor, she paused near the old registration desk.

"We—we saw your truck out front," said the mousy brunette he presumed was Kayla's mother-in-law.

Beside her, the tall gray-haired man Jude assumed was her husband puffed out his chest. "Young lady, we need to speak with you." He glanced Jude's way.

"Is there a problem?" Kayla looked from Joe to Maureen. And since she made no indication for Jude to leave, he stayed put.

The man returned his focus to her. "I believe you've caused our family enough pain."

Nothing like the pain your son inflicted on Kayla, Jude was tempted to say.

Shoulders back, the man continued, "And we are not about to let you cut us out of our grandchild's life."

"I told you I would never do that." Kayla's panicked gaze again bounced from the man to his wife.

"You say that, but you haven't exactly proven yourself to be trustworthy. You decided to stay in Ouray without letting us know *after* you told Maureen she could care for the baby."

"I didn't—"

The jerk cut Kayla off. "At this point, we're not sure you're fit to be a mother. So, with that in mind, we've been discussing our options with an attorney."

Eyes wide, Kayla drew back, hugging her belly protectively. "What does that mean?"

"It means that, as grandparents, we have rights, too." Joe's booming voice held an air of superiority.

The color drained from Kayla's face. And when she stumbled, Jude made sure he was there to steady her. How could these two just waltz in here and treat the woman who was carrying their grandchild like this? Even though Jude suspected the man was making the whole thing up, his words clearly cut Kayla to the quick.

His gaze moved from Kayla to the Bradshaws and back. "I'm sorry, Kayla, but I cannot stand here and let them do this."

He glared at the two people who sought to bully Kayla into doing what *they* wanted. "With all due respect, do you have any idea what your son put Kayla through? What he did to her?" Fury burned within him, but he wouldn't let them know that, especially while he was in uniform. He kept his voice firm, yet even. "Yet, despite everything, she stayed with him, enduring who knows what because she'd made a vow, while he made a mockery of his promise to love and cherish her. *No* woman deserves to be treated the way your son treated Kayla. So how dare you two come in here and threaten her with some bogus claims just to get your way."

Joe stepped closer until he was almost toe-to-toe with Jude. His dark eyes narrowed. "Who are *you* to talk to me this way?"

Though he was only a couple of inches

taller than the man, Jude used it to his advantage. "Someone who's known Kayla for many years. And I will do everything in my power to protect her."

Joe continued to stare, as though waiting to see if Jude was bluffing. But Jude didn't bluff. Especially when it involved someone he loved.

Finally, Joe turned. And without another word, they were gone.

Jude willed himself to calm down before looking at Kayla. When he did, he saw the unshed tears swimming in her chestnut eyes. And the moment her gaze met his, they spilled onto her cheeks.

"What am I going to do, Jude?"

Instinctively, he wrapped his arms around her and held her close. "Nothing. They're just blowing smoke in hopes that they can intimidate you into going back to Denver."

Pulling free, she turned away, hugging her midsection. "How can you say that? This is my baby we're talking about."

He set his hands on her shoulders. "I'm

sorry. I didn't mean to sound so callous." He turned her to face him. "The Bradshaws are acting out of fear and hurt. They lost their son, and they feel like the last piece of him is going to be taken from them, as well. They're desperate. But you can't let them bully you. You have to do what's best for you and the baby."

Shaking her head, she refused to meet his gaze. "I should have never left Denver."

Chapter Fifteen

How could the Bradshaws do this to her?

In the few hours since they'd left, Kayla's emotions had run the gamut. Grief to anger and everything in between. Now, remarkably, her angst had subsided enough to allow rational thinking. Thanks in large part to Jude.

He was right. They were trying to intimidate her in order to get their way.

Looking around the lobby of the now-empty hotel, she wondered what she would have done if he hadn't been here.

After her in-laws left, Jude held her, consoled her and did his best to talk some sense into her. When she refused to listen, he'd called Lily, who'd ultimately talked her off the ledge. Still, it was Jude's presence that had given her the greatest comfort. The man was unshakable, and he seemed to have a knack for being there whenever she needed him.

If only he hadn't kissed her. That one event had messed with her head repeatedly since Sunday. Just because he didn't love her, though, didn't mean he didn't care. And the way he'd stood up for her today endeared him to her more than she was willing to admit. She was falling in love with Jude. But she cherished his friendship too much to let her heart get in the way.

She tucked her latest sketches into a file folder and shoved it into her tote, her resolve suddenly waning. Did her in-laws have any idea how much their words hurt her?

She'd never done anything to indicate that she didn't want her baby to have a relationship with them—quite the contrary. But their behavior these past few days was unnerving, and their desperation was sad.

What if they tried to take your baby?

Her insides twisted. Gripping the edge of the table, she squeezed her eyes shut. She couldn't think like that. She knew in her heart that, with God, all things were possible. And she earnestly prayed that He would change the Bradshaws' minds.

Grabbing her bulky boyfriend sweater from the back of the chair, she shoved her arms into the sleeves. The temperature must be dropping outside because it seemed to be getting colder in here.

The front door opened then, ushering in a blast of cold air. Jude had said he'd be back to check on her, though she hadn't thought that would be so soon.

Turning, she tugged her sweater around her to ward off the chill. But the sight of Maureen Bradshaw sent a shiver slicing through her.

Surprisingly, the woman was alone.

"Where's Joe?" Kayla couldn't help asking.

"Taking a nap at the hotel." Her mother-in-law approached, her smile as nervous as

Kayla felt. "I was hoping you and I could have a talk. Woman to woman."

"About what?" Suspicion narrowed Kayla's gaze.

With a strength she'd rarely seen in her mother-in-law, the woman said, "I'd like you to tell me about my son. Because it appears Joe and I didn't know him at all."

Kayla stood there, blinking. She'd expected another attack, maybe, or even an apology.

Nonetheless, the woman was right. She didn't know her son. At least not the side he so carefully hid from everyone but Kayla.

Kayla pulled out one of the chairs. "Care to sit down?"

"Thank you." While Maureen took her seat, Kayla did the same on the opposite side of the folding table.

She tucked her hair behind her ears and sucked in a shaky breath. "I'm not sure where to start."

Hugging her purse against her chest, the woman said, "How about the beginning?"

Though it had only been six months ago, it felt like a lifetime. Still, if Kayla wanted the Bradshaws to know the truth, she'd have to go back and unearth those things she'd tried so hard to hide. No matter how difficult it might be.

"Shane was one of the kindest people I'd ever known. His gentleness was one of the things I admired most about him and was probably what drew me to him." Hands clasped tightly in her lap, she continued. "I never saw him take a drink until our honeymoon. Normally, he was a very easygoing guy, as you know. Very sweet, loving…" She knew she was rambling, but she couldn't seem to stop. "He had a heart of gold." She hesitated then. "But alcohol turned him into someone I didn't even recognize."

"Did he hurt you?" Lines stretched across Maureen's forehead. "I mean, physically?"

After a long, shame-filled moment, Kayla nodded. "Sometimes. Yes." From there, she went on, revealing painful details of their life together, exposing a side of Shane no one else had ever witnessed.

To her credit, Maureen listened intently, stopping Kayla occasionally to ask questions. Pain flickered in her brown eyes.

"After everything that happened, why didn't you leave him?" she finally asked.

"Honestly, I was planning to. But he died before I could get away."

Maureen reached into her purse and pulled out two tissues. After handing one to Kayla, she dabbed her own eyes with the other. "Sometimes love becomes a choice, doesn't it? When that feeling fades away."

"I'd never thought about it that way, but yes. It did become a choice."

The woman rose then. "I need to get back to Joe."

"Of course." Kayla followed her toward the door, wondering if Maureen believed her or not. She seemed to, but Kayla couldn't get a good read on her.

Maureen stopped then. Turning, she looked at Kayla for the briefest of moments, as though she wanted to say something. Then, without a word, she darted out the door. Leaving Kayla to wonder what would happen next.

Would Maureen and Joe be able to accept the truth about their son?

She'd have to wait and find out because she was too weary to think about it now. Jude would be here soon, and she was ready to call it a day. No telling what he'd have to say when she filled him in on what had just happened.

With her papers already packed, she shuffled across the lobby's wooden floor and headed up to the third floor to turn out the lights. With the assistance of the wooden handrail, she practically dragged herself up the second flight of stairs. A pumpkin spice muffin would be good right about now. Perhaps she'd mix up a batch when she got home. After all, baking was her favorite way to unwind. If she had the strength.

With the third floor shut down, she made her way to the second level and flipped off the light in the hallway before returning to the lobby. Yep, those muffins were sounding better by the—

Two steps into her descent, she lost her footing. Her body swayed this way and that, her arms flailing, trying to catch hold of something but finding nothing. Panic ricocheted through her. Blood roared in her ears. She could not fall. Not now. Not while she was pregnant.

Despite her assertion, the next step drew closer and closer. She reached out a hand to break her fall. Searing pain shot through her wrist. Another thud knocked the wind out of her. White specks shot through her vision.

Thoughts of the tiny life growing inside of her raced through her mind.

God, please protect my baby.

She struggled to wrap her arms around her middle as the freefall continued.

When she hit the bottom, everything went black.

Jude pulled into the hospital parking lot in Montrose before seven thirty the next morning. If he'd had his way, he wouldn't have left last night. And if Kayla hadn't been so adamant, he wouldn't have. It had taken everything within him to walk away while the Bradshaws were still there. No doubt gloating in the fact that Kayla had sent him away.

When he found her unconscious at the bottom of the stairs yesterday, his heart had all but stopped. Thank God the police officer side of him took over because the man who loved her couldn't handle it. He'd radioed dispatch for an ambulance and then spent the next ten excruciating minutes waiting, praying over the woman he loved and the child she carried.

Praise God, she'd come to by the time they'd put her into the ambulance. Something Joe and Maureen had been there to witness. Jude still wasn't sure how he felt about that. A part of him wanted to blame them for what had happened. For upsetting Kayla. But he'd also seen the concern in their eyes as they bombarded him with questions about why she was being taken away.

Later, at the hospital, they'd waited, sharing in his relief when they'd learned both mother and child were doing well. Kayla had suffered a concussion, a broken wrist and some bruising, so the doctor wanted to keep her overnight to monitor her as well as the baby.

As Jude sat with her later, just the two of them, he'd learned that Maureen had returned to the hotel yesterday afternoon to talk with her. He was suspicious, to say the least. He was a cop, after all.

Now, as a new day dawned, all he wanted was to see Kayla and assure himself that she was doing all right. He walked through the automatic sliding doors, leaving a cold rain behind him, and moved into the hospital lobby and straight for the elevator. Too bad the gift shop wasn't open this early. He'd buy her the prettiest bouquet of flowers he could find. Of course, their beauty would pale in comparison to hers.

Standing outside of Kayla's room a few

minutes later, he leaned against the wall, the gravity of her situation slamming into him. His eyes burned as he stared up at the LED lights.

God, thank You for protecting her. I'm not sure I could face losing her again.

With a deep breath, he continued into her room.

The rhythmic hum and click of an IV pump sifted through the silence. A blanket covered Kayla's legs while her casted arm rested atop her unborn child. The head of the bed was elevated, her dark hair a stark contrast to the white sheets. For a moment, he thought she was asleep, but as he drew closer, he saw she was simply staring out the partially opened blinds.

As though sensing his presence, she turned and looked up at him, her chestnut eyes lacking their usual sparkle. "Morning."

"How are you feeling?" Longing to touch her, he gripped the side rail instead.

"Okay, I guess. My head's still throbbing."

He eyed the contusion just above her

temple. "No doubt. You hit it pretty hard." If only he'd been there to catch her. His gaze lowered. "How's the baby doing?"

The corners of her mouth lifted then as she smoothed her good hand over the blanket. "Very active."

"That's good to hear."

"Yeah. I think he or she is trying to get back at me for all the jostling yesterday."

"Ah, a little payback, huh?"

Nodding, she focused on her hands. "Jude, there's something I need to tell you."

"Sure."

She took a deep breath and exhaled before peering up at him. "I had a long talk with Joe and Maureen last night. They believe everything I told them about Shane, and I now understand why they said all the things they did."

"Why?"

"Because they were hurting. Shane was their only child. This baby means a lot to them."

"Oh, so that gives them the right to threaten you?"

She lowered her head. "I've decided to go back to Denver and live with them until the baby is born."

His hold on the side rail tightened. This had to be the Bradshaws' doing. No wonder they'd stayed last night. "Was this their idea?"

"No." Her gaze remained riveted to his. "It was mine."

Suddenly, he found himself struggling for air. As though he'd been punched in the gut. "Why?"

"Because I almost lost my baby yesterday, and I'm not willing to risk going through that again."

Her logic was a little misguided, perhaps, but he supposed he understood. "You'll be coming back, though? After the baby arrives."

She stared at her hands again. "I honestly don't know."

"But what about the hotel? Have you talked to Lily?"

"Yes. She understands."

Good. Maybe she could explain it to him.

Frustrated, he shoved a hand through his hair. Whether Kayla wanted to admit it or not, the Bradshaws had indeed gotten to her. All of their guilt trips and threats had worked to undermine the confidence she'd been working so hard to regain. Now she was afraid to trust herself with her own well-being and that of her child, putting her right back where she'd been when Shane was alive.

He glanced at her. Saw the pain in her eyes. In that moment, he realized the cycle that had filtered its way through the Bradshaw family. Joe was used to bullying people, including his family, to achieve whatever outcome he wanted. His wife and his son had been impacted. And though Shane may have been decent when he was sober, the alcohol turned him into a much more aggressive version of his father.

Well, Jude wasn't about to let that cycle impact Kayla or her baby anymore.

He wrapped his fingers around those on her good hand and smiled down at her. "Marry me, Kayla. Stay with me in Ouray.

I promise, I will take such good care of you and the baby."

Surprise widened her eyes, and her mouth opened ever so slightly. Finally, she squeezed his fingers, then released them. "You're so sweet, but that wouldn't be fair to you."

Not fair? What did that mean?

She doesn't love you.

The aching sensation he'd never wanted to feel again filled him as the thought sank in. Of course, she didn't love him. Her husband hadn't even been gone six months.

"Yeah, that probably wasn't my best idea. But why don't I hang around and give you a ride home once the doctor sets you free? I mean, they're probably not going to want you to travel for a while."

"No, they won't. Lily's planning to take me back to Ouray."

"Oh. Okay." Except it wasn't okay. Nothing was okay. He was losing Kayla again. Correction. He'd already lost her. "I guess I'll let you get some rest then."

An aide whisked into the room, carrying a breakfast tray.

Jude pressed a kiss against Kayla's silky hair, savoring the delicate aroma of her one last time. "You've got my number. Memorize it this time. And don't ever hesitate to call."

She smiled as he pulled away. "I won't."

With that, he turned and walked out of the room, feeling as though his insides had been shredded to pieces. The only woman he'd ever loved was gone. Again. And he didn't have a clue how to get her back.

He made his way back down to the lobby and out the door, sorrow wrapping around him like a cold, wet blanket. Where did he go from here? What would he do?

Not watching where he was going as he exited the hospital, he almost bumped into the Bradshaws.

"Good morning, Jude." Holding an umbrella, Maureen was all smiles. Why wouldn't she be? Kayla was returning to Denver. To live with them, no less. "How's our girl doing this morning?"

Our girl? Kayla may not be his, but she certainly wasn't theirs either.

"She's improving."

"Good." Hands shoved in the pockets of his work pants, Joe looked him in the eye. "I—uh, wanted to thank you for standing up to us—me—and speaking on Kayla's behalf." He glanced at his wife before continuing. "If you hadn't, we might never have known the truth about our son." He cleared his throat. "I only wish I could have protected Kayla."

They believed her? That was unexpected. As was their gratitude.

"It's obvious you care for her very much," Joe added.

"Yes, sir." More than anyone would ever know. And he could only pray that, after the baby was born, Kayla would return to Ouray and give him the opportunity to prove himself once again.

Chapter Sixteen

Kayla would do anything to protect her baby, no matter what the cost to her. Even if it meant saying goodbye to the man she'd fallen in love with for a second time.

Watching raindrops pelt the window of her hospital room, she swiped a tear from her cheek. Her breakfast tray sat untouched, her appetite gone, right along with Jude. Though the latter was probably for the better. The longer he stayed, the more likely she was to fall apart.

Seemed that, despite her insistence that Jude was only a friend, her heart had other plans. She'd gotten used to having him in her life again. Enjoyed it, even. The way he encouraged her, talked her through her troubles, helped her discover what *she* really wanted. Most of all, he made her feel safe.

But even Jude couldn't protect her from everything.

Revealing her plans to him had been more heartrending than she'd expected. If only his proposal had been real. Not that he wasn't sincere. His loyalty and protectiveness were two of his greatest qualities. Jude wanted to shield her from the Bradshaws. She got that. But she couldn't marry someone who didn't love her.

Besides, the Bradshaws really did care about her. After Jude left last night, they'd apologized for what they'd put her through, as well as what Shane had done. Not only were they deeply troubled to learn the truth about their son, they'd vowed to make amends for his actions any way they could.

That's when Kayla knew what she had to do. Because the thought of something else happening that could jeopardize her baby was too much to bear. She asked them if she could live with them until the baby was born, and they'd agreed.

Memories of tumbling down those stairs yesterday had her hugging her belly. Just the thought of what could have happened had tears stinging her eyes. *Thank You, God, for protecting my baby. And me.*

"Good morning, dear." Maureen walked into the room with Joe on her heels.

Kayla sniffed and quickly freed her hands from beneath the blanket to swipe away any trace of tears while her mother-in-law hurriedly placed her purse in the chair near the window and shrugged out of her coat.

Pausing at the foot of her bed, hands shoved in the pockets of his work pants, Joe appeared uncomfortable. As though he didn't know what to say.

Finally, he shrugged and said, "How are you?"

The fact that he asked about her and not simply the baby warmed her heart. "Doing better." She smoothed a hand over her belly. "However, I think someone is practicing to be a kicker for the Broncos."

That brought a smile to the oft-grouchy face of her father-in-law. He really could be a bit of a softy, though he preferred to hide beneath his tough exterior.

Maureen lifted the lid on Kayla's food tray, releasing the nauseating smell of scrambled eggs and sausage.

Kayla's stomach churned.

Frowning, Maureen said, "You haven't touched your breakfast, dear."

"I'm not very hungry."

"But what about the baby?" The woman stared at her very matter-of-factly. "The little one needs all the nutrition he or she can get for those growing bones and muscles."

Kayla got that. But nothing sounded good.

"At least drink your milk." The woman picked up the glass and passed it to Kayla.

Why not? After all, that's what she'd settled on after passing out at Lily's wedding. That had been the first time she'd felt the baby kick, and Jude had been there to share the milestone with her. She recalled the look of wonder on his face as he reveled in that special moment.

Shoving the thought aside, she accepted the cup and took a drink while Maureen retrieved her phone and poked at the screen. "I was thinking that it might be nice to turn Shane's room into a nursery."

"Oh," was all Kayla could manage as she struggled to wrap her aching head around the idea.

"Yes, but it's been so long since I've had a baby." Maureen tapped at her phone screen again. "So, I went to the internet to look for some inspiration. There we go." She handed the phone to Kayla. "What would you think about something like this?"

She peered at the image on the screen. Surprisingly, it looked very similar to the nursery Lily had described the day Kayla moved into Livie's House. Lots of natural light, greige walls, white crib—

Her heart plummeted then. Jude's crib. He'd put so much thought into it. First sketching out designs he thought she'd like, then getting the end pieces ready for her to see last Sunday.

Her fingers automatically went to her lips. That was the same day he'd kissed her. And for one amazing moment she'd been able to let go of everything else and dare to dream.

Funny how life could change so quickly. She should be used to it by now.

"Do you like it?" Maureen waited hopefully.

Kayla cleared her throat. "I do. Yeah, it's very pretty."

"And so stylish." Maureen reclaimed her phone. "Reminds of something that couple on HGTV would do."

"Just don't be getting ideas about taking down any walls." Joe eyed them both.

While Maureen laughed him off, Kayla stared into her half-empty glass. What was wrong with her? She should be excited about her baby's nursery. Shouldn't she?

Instead, all she could think about was Jude and the hotel. There was so much she was going to miss about Ouray.

And what about Lily? She'd given Kayla the opportunity of a lifetime. Now Kayla was letting her down.

Two raps on the door had Kayla looking that way as Lily breezed into the room. "Good morning, everyone." A stylish saddle-brown tote purse hung from one elbow while her other hand held a foil pan encased in a clear plastic bag. "I brought you a present," she continued in a singsong voice as she approached Kayla and set the pan in her lap.

Kayla stared at it, her appetite suddenly returning. "Cinnamon rolls?"

"From Granny's Kitchen, of course."

Kayla undid the twist tie, allowing the sweet aroma to escape. "They smell divine."

Lily crossed to the food tray, dumped the toast from the plate and handed it to Kayla along with a fork. "Here you go."

"Thanks." Kayla scooped a roll onto the plate before handing the pan back to her friend.

"There's plenty for everyone." Lily looked from Maureen to Joe.

Another rap at the door ushered in Kayla's doctor. "Well, it certainly smells good in here."

Kayla swallowed her first gooey bite. "Care for a cinnamon roll?"

Clad in a white lab coat, Dr. Lawrence eyed her plate as he approached. "Now that's tempting."

A smiling Lily held up the pan. "We have extras."

He adjusted the stethoscope around his neck. "You ladies drive a hard bargain, but I'm afraid I'd be taking my life in my own hands if I walked out of here with one of those and didn't have any for the nurses."

"Good point." Lily set the pan atop the bedside table. "Next time I'll bring two pans."

The doctor flipped through the pages on Kayla's chart. "Everything looks good. Baby's healthy, so I'm going to go ahead and discharge you. However, no traveling for a week, and I'd prefer you not be alone for another twenty-four to forty-eight hours."

Out of the corner of her eye, Kayla saw Maureen open her mouth. Yet before she could say anything, Lily piped up.

"I'm planning to stay with her."

"You are?" Kayla couldn't help her surprise.

"Why wouldn't I? I'm the overprotective big sister, remember?"

Yeah, who had a brand-new husband and two kids to care for, among other things. And she was Kayla's birthing coach. Except Lily would be in Ouray while Kayla would be Denver. Who would be her birthing coach then?

She glanced at her mother-in-law.

Kayla was *not* comfortable with that scenario. But who else was there? Was she destined to deliver this baby alone?

What little breakfast she'd eaten turned into a lead weight in her stomach.

God, am I really doing the right thing by going back to Denver?

* * *

Jude didn't think it was possible to feel any worse than he had when Kayla drove away from Ouray seven years ago. Then she dumped him—or so he thought—and he lost all contact with her. Knowing she was gone for good had left his heart battered and scarred.

Still, none of that compared to what he was feeling now. Since leaving the hospital this morning, a deep, burrowing ache had wormed itself throughout his entire being. Just the simple act of breathing was almost more than he could bear. So, as night fell, he did the only thing he knew to do. He escaped to his shop and prayed everyone would leave him alone and let him ride out this latest storm all by himself.

Standing at his workbench, he picked up one of the end pieces of the crib he'd started for Kayla. He smoothed his hand over the grain, thinking about the light that had sparkled in her eyes when he'd shown her. And the way she'd fit so perfectly in his arms when he'd kissed her. That kiss had held so much promise.

How could things have gone so wrong?

The door opened then, and Jude cringed. He didn't want to see anybody, let alone talk to anyone. He glanced up to see his father coming toward him.

"Jude, we need to talk cattle."

Great. The topic he'd been avoiding ever since the first time the old man brought it up.

His father stopped in front of him, his brow furrowing as he looked Jude in the eye. "Something's wrong. Is Kayla all right? The baby?"

Setting the crib piece aside, Jude crossed his arms and leaned against the workbench. "They're both fine."

"Whew. You had me worried for a minute." His gaze narrowed on Jude, concern weighing heavy in his dark eyes. "What's troubling you, son?"

Suddenly Jude felt more like a boy than a man. "I lost her, Dad." He swallowed the lump that had settled in his throat. "Again."

"Kayla?"

He nodded. "She's decided to return to Denver and live with her in-laws."

"Forever?"

"She says until the baby's born."

"Is she coming back then? What about the hotel?"

"At this point, she's not sure. All I know is that I blew it."

"Why do you say that?"

He didn't realize he'd picked a game of twenty questions. Lowering his arms, he moved to the opposite side of the bench. "I asked her to marry me, and she said no, all right."

"What do you mean, you—" Thumbs dangling from his belt loops, the old man followed him, shaking his head. "I don't know why it is you and your brothers— Matt anyway—think you can just up and propose in some last-ditch effort to hold on to the women you love."

"What are you talking about?"

"Did you tell Kayla you love her?"

He thought for a moment, shifting from

one booted foot to the other. "Okay, so I might have failed to mention that, but I promised to take care of her and the baby."

"Son, women need to know they're loved. They want to see it as well as hear it. A man can tell a woman he loves her all day long, but if it doesn't come through in his actions, she's not going to believe him."

Sounded like Kayla's late husband. "Mama always said love is an action verb."

"That's right. And I never had a problem showing your mama I loved her. Providing for her, caring for her, doing little things without her asking. Then, one day, she looked at me said, 'Tell me you love me.'" Leaning his backside against the workbench, he crossed his feet at the ankles. "I couldn't understand it. I said, 'You know I love you.' To which she responded, 'Then why is it so difficult for you to say?'"

Mama was never afraid to call his father out. Kind of like Hillary. "What did you do?"

"Well, after I swallowed my pride, I took

her in my arms, told her I loved her, then gave her a kiss that took her breath away."

Jude puffed out a laugh. "You know, you really didn't need to share that last part."

Dad's brow lifted in irritation. "Yeah, well, deal with it." He fell quiet for a moment. "When you and Kayla split, you were so heartbroken your mom was afraid you'd give up on finding love."

"I didn't give up. It was just that the bar had been set so high. Kayla got me in a way no one else ever had. We complemented each other. And she was the prettiest carpenter I've ever known."

Dad grinned. "You sure you haven't given up now? Because you're talking in the past tense, as though Kayla is already gone."

Jude shoved a hand through his hair. "I don't know what I'm doing, Dad." He stepped away from the bench and turned to face his father. "However, there is something I need to talk to you about."

"Go ahead."

"I hate to disappoint you, but I don't want to be a cattle rancher."

The old man simply stared.

"Woodworking is my passion." Jude gestured throughout the shop. "And it's providing me with more income than I ever imagined. I'm sorry, but I can't give up on my dream. I just hope you can understand that."

His father nodded. "I know you and your brothers think I'm stubborn and set in my ways, but I do understand. And I'm proud of you for standing up to me and telling me the truth."

"You are?"

"Of course, I am. My dad thought I was crazy when I told him I wanted to be a cattle rancher, but he still respected my decision."

"Does this mean you think I'm crazy?"

"A little, maybe." The old man winked. "Though I am curious 'bout something." He straightened and crossed to one of the inventory shelves where he picked up a baluster. "Just how much are you making from all this wood?"

The old man's eyes grew wide when Jude told him what his income had been last year. "Why didn't you tell me that in the first place? Good night." Setting the wood piece back in the box, he shoved his hands into the pockets of his worn Wranglers and ambled back toward Jude. "You'd be crazy to give up that kind of money. Especially when you love what you're doing."

"What are you going to do about the cattle operation, though?"

"Well…" His father tilted his Stetson back and scratched his head. "I reckon it's my turn to fess up now."

"What do you mean?"

"Jude, I actually came in here to tell you I've changed my mind."

"Changed your mind? Why?"

"When I told Hillary I was planning to turn the operation over to you, she told me I was crazy."

Jude laughed. He could hear her saying just that.

"She wanted to know why I was giving up something that meant so much to me. When I told her I was doing it for her, because I thought she might want to travel or live in town, she glared at me and told me she loves me just the way I am and that I'd better not change a thing."

"That's great, Dad." Jude could hardly believe that his father had been willing to sacrifice his dream—everything—for love. What had he ever sacrificed for love?

Nothing, except love itself.

The thought prodded him the rest of the night. In particular, the word *sacrifice*, but it wasn't until he crawled into bed he understood why. He flipped on his lamp and riffled through the top drawer of his bedside stand until he found the envelope that contained a note from his mother. One she'd written shortly before she died.

Pulling out the card adorned with a columbine, he opened it and read.

My beloved Jude,
The time we shared at the beginning of
your life and the end of mine are some
of my most cherished memories. With
five years between you and Matt, I was
able to sit and hold my infant son to my
heart's content. Years later, when I got
sick, you were there for me. Whether I
needed a helping hand or just someone
to sit with me, I could always count on
you.

He briefly closed his eyes, trying to hold
back the emotions that threatened.

Your loyalty is one of your greatest
traits. But it also holds you back from
following your dreams. Don't give up
on your dreams, Jude. In life or in love.
Yes, it sometimes involves sacrifice,
but it's almost always worth it. The
Bible tells us love always protects, always trusts, always hopes, always perseveres. Whatever you long for, Jude,
keep at it. Don't ever give up.

Thoughts of Kayla played across his mind. He'd dreamed of being with her, building a life with her almost all of his adult life, but what had he ever done to make that dream become a reality?

Nothing.

His father was right. He'd given up. Both then and now. And that had to change because no sacrifice was too great for Kayla. He couldn't give up hope. He would persevere.

Chapter Seventeen

Kayla ended the call with her mother, feeling more than a little conflicted.

Fingering the sheer curtain out of the way, she watched the snow fall over Ouray Friday afternoon. It felt good to be back in her own house. Well, not exactly hers, but Livie's House was home nonetheless. For a few more days anyway.

When she'd returned yesterday, she'd been overwhelmed by the generosity of the townsfolk. She hadn't been in Ouray long enough to really get to know anyone outside of Jude's family, yet a steady flow of people, many of whom were strangers, had streamed in and out of her house all afternoon. Folks brought soups, casseroles, desserts…

Hillary's daughter, Celeste Purcell, who was also expecting a baby in February, had dropped off cinnamon rolls and a hearty beef stew. This morning, Carly had come by with pumpkin muffins and quiche. And Lacie had stopped in just before lunch with some chocolate cupcakes. Considering Lacie had been battling morning sickness, Kayla felt extra blessed to receive those.

She'd never seen such an outpouring of kindness, let alone been the beneficiary. Not in all her years growing up on the road or when her father was sick or even when Shane died. Lily said that's just how people were in Ouray. All Kayla knew was that it was going to make leaving this tiny town with a great big heart even more difficult.

"Hey, you're supposed to be on the couch."

Turning, she spotted Lily coming out of the kitchen, holding two white mugs. "I wanted to see the snow."

"Don't give me that." Wearing a cream-colored cowl-neck tunic sweater over skinny jeans, Lily eased across the wooden planks. "You can see it from the sofa."

"Not with these sheers filtering my view."

"Fine." Lily set the mugs on the coffee table before coming alongside Kayla. She slid the panels left and right, leaving an unobstructed view. "Happy now?"

"Yes, thank you." Smiling at her friend, she returned to the sofa. "Ooo, hot chocolate." She reached for one whipped-cream-topped cup, then sank onto the plush gray sofa, tucking her sock-covered feet beneath her. "You know, for an annoying big sister, you do a pretty good job of spoiling me."

"Some people are worth spoiling." Lily grabbed her own drink and joined Kayla on the couch. "Besides, this particular indulgence benefits me, too." She lifted her mug in salute before taking a sip.

Kayla sure was going to miss her friend. Not to mention Jude. Actually, she missed him already. There had been a finality to his goodbye yesterday, and she knew she wouldn't see him again before she left—if ever, since she was still undecided as to what to do, where to go, after the baby came.

She'd contemplated calling him, just to hear his voice, but decided against it. What was the point? She'd made her decision. She had to do what was best for her baby.

So why was she still plagued with all this confusion?

Because only a few days ago, you were embracing a new beginning in Ouray. New town, new home, new job...

"What did your mom have to say?" Lily watched her from the opposite end of the sofa.

"Just that she was glad I was back in Ouray and that you were with me and that she'd been praying."

"What did she say about your decision to move in with the Bradshaws?"

"I think she was a little surprised, but after the initial shock wore off, she agreed that I needed to do what's right for me and the baby."

"I thought she might offer to come up here and stay with you herself."

"And leave her sailor man? I don't think so." Though it would have been nice. She wrapped her hands tighter around her mug, savoring its warmth. "I didn't tell you this, but Jude asked me to marry him."

"What?" Lily's green eyes went wide. She straightened and set her cup on the side table. "When?"

"Yesterday morning, before anyone else had arrived at the hospital." She lifted a shoulder. "It wasn't a real proposal, though. He only wanted to protect me from the Bradshaws."

"Are you sure it was just that?" Her friend's brow arched. "You don't think it could have been because he *wants* you to stay in Ouray?"

Kayla swirled her spoon through her drink. "Why would he care if I stayed or not?"

"I can't believe you even have to ask that." Her friend shot her an annoyed look.

"It's obvious that Jude loves you and wants to pursue a relationship with you."

"Yeah, right." Kayla knew for a fact that Jude did not love her. He'd told her himself right after he kissed her, apologizing for getting caught up in the emotion of the day as if that was supposed to make everything all right.

"Say what you want, but it's written all over his face whenever he sees you, Kayla. The gleam in his eye, smiling for no particular reason…" Lily retrieved her drink and leaned back. "And honestly, I think you might be in love with him, too."

Kayla puffed out a laugh, nearly choking on the sip she'd just taken. "I'm not even sure I know what love is. I mean, I thought I loved Shane. But if that's the case, why didn't I grieve his death?" She looked toward the other end of the sofa. "All I ever felt was relief."

Tenderness filled her friend's gaze. "Sweetie, you did love Shane, but he betrayed that love, just like Wade betrayed me. The only difference was that Shane's mistress came in a bottle. Betrayal erodes the trust we placed in that person. And in your case, it made you fearful. That's where the relief came in. It doesn't mean you didn't love him. You simply weren't afraid anymore."

While that made sense... "But Shane's been gone less than six months. How could I possibly be in love with someone else, as you suggested?"

"I fell in love with Noah in less than two months, and I didn't even know him. You and Jude have a history. You know the kind of man he is, his character. That's why you fell in love with him the first time."

Yes, it was. And now, as she looked toward a future without him in it, it was becoming more and more apparent that she had indeed fallen in love with him again. His belief in her had gone a long way toward helping her regain faith in herself. He encouraged her and made her feel safe. He was everything she wanted in a man.

Except he didn't love her.

"I just hope I'm making the right decision."

"Turning down Jude's proposal?"

She looked at her friend. "No, moving in with the Bradshaws."

"I thought it was your idea."

"It was." Lifting a shoulder, she eyed her friend, guilt weighing heavily. "What are you going to do about the hotel?"

Lily drew in a breath laced with disappointment. "If you decide not to come back, I guess I'll have to find another general contractor." She shrugged. "It won't be the same, though." She took a sip.

The ache in Kayla's heart intensified. Even though Lily understood why Kayla had to return to Denver, Kayla was letting her down. Like Jude, Lily believed in her. Trusted her and was counting on her to do the job.

"I completed all of my sketches. All I need to do is finish up the designs on my computer. I can do that in Denver and then email them to you so you'll have everything you need."

"I know." Lily smiled and patted Kayla's leg.

Downing the rest of her cocoa, Kayla set her mug aside. "It's strange, yesterday I was confident that I was making the right decision, but now that I'm out of the hospital... I don't know. Being here just feels so right."

Lily reached for her hand. "Sweetie, maybe that's because it is."

After a restless night, Jude had spent all morning working on the plan he'd come up with somewhere between midnight and 2:00 a.m. This time, he would not let Kayla go without a fight.

Now, with the lunch crowd long gone, he slid into a window-side booth at Granny's Kitchen and met the confused gazes of Joe and Maureen Bradshaw on the opposite side of the table.

"Thank you both for agreeing to meet me."

"Is something wrong with Kayla?" Maureen's dark eyes narrowed in concern.

"No, ma'am. Not that I'm aware of." Seeing their angst, he decided it was best to get to the point. "I just wanted to let you both know that I'm planning to move to Denver to be near Kayla." Since she would be living with them, he thought it only right to let the Bradshaws know about his plans.

The couple exchanged a look he couldn't interpret, the way his parents so often had. As though having a private discussion without ever saying a word.

"You know she's only been widowed for six months," Joe finally said.

Hands clasped atop the glossy wooden tabletop, Jude met the man's gaze. "That is something that played heavily into my decision." He shifted in his seat. "You see, Kayla and I met seven years ago—long before she met your son—when she and her parents lived in Ouray for a short time, and I've been in love with her ever since."

"I assume things didn't work out?" Joe continued to watch him.

"No. Her parents left, she went with them, and due to some unfortunate miscommunication, we lost contact. And I've been kicking myself ever since for letting her go. That's a mistake I'm not willing to make again."

Maureen leaned closer. "You're willing to wait, though?"

"Yes, ma'am. As long as it takes."

"What if things don't turn out the way you hope?" Joe reached for his half-full coffee cup. "What if Kayla doesn't feel the same way about you?"

That was a question Jude had been trying to ignore. Though, deep inside, he knew the possibility was all too real. "Then at least I will know that I tried."

The two looked at each other again.

Once again, Joe addressed him. "I realize we don't know you, Jude. However, in the few times our paths have crossed, you've shown yourself to be more than a little protective of Kayla."

"I'm willing to give up my life here to do just that. Like the Bible says, love always protects, trusts, hopes and perseveres. And that's exactly what I intend to do."

Another look passed between Joe and Maureen before Joe extended a hand across the table. "Jude, you're welcome in our home anytime."

Jude left the restaurant, feeling as though a weight had been lifted from his shoulders. But he wasn't done yet. There was still one final step he had to take.

He climbed into his truck and drove the two blocks to his grandmother's house. Snow fell at a steady rate, however he doubted they'd have much accumulation. Sure was pretty to look at, though.

A few moments later, he made his way up the front walk and stood outside of Kayla's door. His heart hung in his throat, and he tried in vain to swallow around it. *Lord, don't let me mess this up. Please.*

The door opened before he even knocked.

"Jude?" Lily motioned for him to come inside. "I thought that was you moving past the window."

Glancing to his right, he saw the curtains spread wide. "Yep, that was me, all right." He swept a hand across his hair to remove any trace of snow, his gaze drifting to the couch where Kayla was curled up in one

corner, wearing a gray Ouray sweatshirt
and black leggings, a mixture of emotions
playing across her beautiful face.

"Hi," he managed to eke out.

"Hi." The corners of her mouth twitched.

"And on that note—" Lily snatched up
her coat from the side chair "—I'm going
to run up to the school to meet the kids
when they get out." She shoved her arms
into the sleeves. "Jude, would you mind
watching over the patient while I'm gone?
Make sure she doesn't try to run any mar-
athons or anything."

He smiled at his new sister-in-law. "Take
all the time you need, Lily."

Armed with a knowing grin, the woman
grabbed her purse and headed out the door.

Hands shoved in the pockets of his coat,
he eased toward the sofa, his heart beat-
ing a million miles a minute. "Mind if I
join you?"

"Of course not." Kayla motioned to the
space beside her.

He drank in the sight of her as he sat.
While the bruise on her forehead remained

a deep purple, the color had returned to her cheeks. Her silky dark hair spilled over her shoulders. Man, she was gorgeous.

He swiped his sweaty palms across his jeans and sucked in a deep breath.

"Jude, please say whatever it is you came to say, because you're making me nervous."

Twisting, he reached for her hand. "Sorry, I didn't mean—" He let go a sigh, allowing his gaze to hone in on her beautiful chestnut eyes. "Kayla, I let you walk out of my life once, and I'm not about to let that happen again. I came here to tell you that I'm moving to Denver, too. I've already talked to the Bradshaws, and they're—"

"Wait!" Kayla held up a hand. "Why would you do that? What about your business?"

"Andrew has a buddy who's willing to lease me some space in his warehouse. My business will be going with me."

"But what about Ouray? You love it here. This is where your roots are."

He squeezed her hand. "Kayla, I'd rather sacrifice that than live with regrets and what-ifs again. I know you need time. And I'm willing to give you all the time you need because I love you, Kayla. I always have." He puffed out a laugh. "I wanted to marry you seven years ago, and that desire is just as strong now as it was then."

Her chestnut eyes widened. "Then how come you never asked me?"

"How could I? You liked your nomadic life. I was afraid my need for roots would stifle you and you'd grow to hate me."

"Oh, Jude." She shook her head, her long hair swaying from side to side. "You don't know how hard I prayed that you *would* ask me to stay?"

Now he was confused. "Really?"

"I fell in love with Ouray that summer. And you."

"You—you mean you wanted to stay?"

"More than anything."

Brushing her hair behind her ear, he

stared into those eyes that had plagued his dreams for years. "Kayla, I've never stopped loving you. Even when we lost contact. Even when I thought you were married. You're the only woman I've ever wanted, and it would make me the happiest man alive to have you as my wife. But I'm willing to wait until you're ready. No matter how long it takes."

"Oh, Jude." A tear spilled onto her cheek. "I do love you."

He wiped it away with his thumb before touching his lips to hers.

Her arms wound around his neck, her kiss full of hope and longing. And he savored every moment with this amazing woman.

A knock on the door had him abruptly pulling away. "You expecting someone?"

She shook her head. "Unless it's someone else bringing food."

Clearing his throat, he stood and smoothed a hand over his hair. After glancing Kayla's way to make sure she was ready, he opened the door.

"Joe. Maureen." He held the door as they entered.

Kayla started to stand, but Maureen scurried to stop her.

"No, no, dear. You sit." The woman eased beside her and looked in Joe's direction.

He'd assumed his usual stance, hands buried in his pockets. "We stopped by to let you know we're heading back to Denver."

Kayla's confused gazed darted between them. "I didn't realize you were leaving so soon." For a moment, she looked torn. Then she squared her shoulders and said, "If you don't mind, though, I think I'd like to stay in Ouray. For good."

Joe nodded. "I don't see why not." He looked from his wife to Kayla. "Seems like a nice little community. Good place to raise a child."

Maureen's sad smile was filled with warmth. "It'll give you that fresh start you've been wanting." The woman faced Jude then. "Besides, we have every confidence that you'll be in *very* good hands."

Chapter Eighteen

This was the day. Kayla knew what she wanted, and she was ready to go for it.

Armed with hot pads, she opened the oven door at Livie's House and pulled out the casserole dish holding her favorite corn pudding. The recipe had been her father's favorite and was a staple at every Thanksgiving and Christmas dinner.

Carly was preparing the bulk of the Thanksgiving meal, which would be held next door at Granger House Inn—very convenient, should Kayla need to slip away to rest—so the least Kayla could do was offer to bring a side dish.

She set the casserole atop the stove and

covered it with a lid, excited to be spending her first holiday with the Stephens family. A large family gathered around the table... She and Lily agreed that was something they were both looking forward to. Something they'd dreamed of as only children.

At least Lily bore the Stephens last name—a distinction Kayla hoped to achieve very soon.

In the meantime, she would delight in the fact that, for the first time in her life, she felt at home. Content and blessed beyond belief. Seven years ago, she'd had a feeling about Ouray. Now she knew it to be true. Ouray was where she belonged. Ouray was her home.

And while a handsome woodworker may have had something to do with that feeling, the people of Ouray had played a bigger role. They'd embraced her, welcomed her, prayed for her...

Those prayers had healed her in more ways than she ever would have thought possible. By God's grace, she felt renewed. More certain of herself and what she wanted out of life. No more indecision. Ouray was where she wanted to be, and Jude was the man she wanted to spend the rest of her life with. His chivalry may have bugged her when she first returned, but, in the long run, it was one of the things she appreciated most about him and had grown to count on.

If only she hadn't hesitated on putting in an offer for the old Orr house. By the time she came to her senses, it was already under contract with someone else.

With the casserole ready and waiting, she went into the bedroom to check her look in the full-length mirror. Thanks to her ever-growing waistline, she was no longer able to wear her overalls to work at the hotel. Still, the stylish dress and boots she wore today were far more feminine than her usual sweatshirt and leggings.

Two weeks ago, she'd submitted all of the drawings and applications for permits on the hotel. And last week, she'd picked up the actual permits, meaning work could finally begin on the new and improved

Congress Hotel. She could hardly wait to get started. And since she had hired most of her crew, she wouldn't have to wait long.

She looked at her watch. Where was Jude? She thought he'd be here by now. She was hoping for a few minutes alone with him before they went next door.

Just then, a rap sounded at the door.

After one last look in the mirror, she drew in a deep breath and moved into the living room. This was it.

She continued across the large area rug, pulled the door open and nearly choked. Jude always looked good to her, but today he appeared especially fine. Clean-shaven, freshly trimmed hair—was that a new shirt? She didn't recall seeing that particular blue-gray combo before.

"Happy Thanksgiving." He smiled and paused for a brief kiss as he entered.

"Happy Thanksgiving to you." She pressed a hand against his chest, feeling the taut muscles beneath the button-down.

"Smells good in here." He moved toward the kitchen. "Are you ready to go?"

She hurried behind him. "No, not yet. We still have a few minutes."

Turning, he wrapped his arms around her waist. "You okay? You seem a little nervous."

"Me? Nervous?" Whatever would she have to be nervous about? It wasn't like she was about to turn the tables and propose to him or anything. But given that he'd left things kind of open-ended, pretty much leaving it up to her to decide when she was ready to discuss marriage...

"Yes." He eyed her suspiciously. "What's going on?"

Oh, she might as well just get it over with.

She slipped her arms around his neck, savoring his nearness as she stared into his gorgeous dark eyes. "Jude, will you marry me?"

A slow grin split his face as he tugged her closer. But he had yet to say anything.

Now she really was nervous.

"After Shane died, I told myself I'd never fall in love again. I was afraid to trust my judgment. But because of you, my faith in myself and love has been restored. You are unchanging. Your character is the same today as it was when we met all those years ago. And despite what I told myself, I have fallen in love with you."

Again, he just smiled. It was getting annoying.

Finally, he said, "I love you, too. But—" He removed his hands from her waist and took a step back.

"But what?" Oh, no. There wasn't supposed to be a *but*.

Tears pricked the backs of her eyes. She looked at the ceiling and blinked. She would not cry—not unless they were happy tears.

"But," he said again, "you can't have a proper proposal without a ring."

What?

She lowered her gaze to discover him kneeling before her, still smiling, and holding the most beautiful engagement ring she'd ever seen. A brilliant princess-cut solitaire surrounded by a halo of smaller diamonds.

"Kayla Bradshaw, will you marry me?"

As tears began to stream down her face, she almost said yes. Then caught herself. "I asked you first."

He chuckled. "Yes, Kayla, I will most definitely marry you." He pushed to his feet and slipped the ring on the fourth finger of her left hand. "Not only do I want to share my life with you, I want to love this child growing inside of you now and look forward to more babies with you." His arms moved around her waist again, and he pulled her closer. "It's your turn now."

With her heart full to overflowing and tears still falling, she could only manage one word. "Yes."

He lowered his head and kissed her thoroughly before pulling away and staring into her eyes. "I have something else for you, too."

"Oh?" She couldn't imagine what it could be. She already had everything she'd ever wanted. Everything she ever dreamed of.

Reaching around his back, he pulled out a thick envelope and handed it to her.

She looked from the envelope to him. "What's this?"

"Open it and find out."

She slid a finger under the flap and pulled out the tri-folded paperwork, curiously peering up at him. Opening it, she realized it was a contract of some sort. She quickly scanned the page. "This looks like a purchase agreement for the old Orr house." Confused, she looked up at him again. "But somebody already bought it."

"Apparently, the contract fell through. The listing agent called me this morning to let me know it was back on the market."

"Why would she do that?"

He grinned. "Perhaps someone put a bug in her ear to keep me informed should something like that happen."

Her heart melted. Could she possibly love this man more? "You did that for me?"

"I know how much you love that house." He fingered the paperwork in her hands. "I picked up the offer agreement on my way over here. Once we both sign it, she can present it to the owner."

"Oh, Jude." She threw her arms around his neck and kissed him with abandon. In one single day, this incredible man had made all of her dreams come true. "This is, without a doubt, the best Thanksgiving ever."

"One more push, Kayla. Come on, you can do it." With one hand in his wife's death grip and the other pressed against her back, Jude did his best to encourage her as she fought to bring their first child into the world.

Sweat dripped from Kayla's brow as she let out a guttural groan one more time.

Seconds later, a tiny cry echoed throughout the birthing room.

"It's a girl!" The doctor held her tiny body up for them to see.

"We have a daughter." Jude kissed his exhausted wife.

Still trying to catch her breath, Kayla

said, "I can't believe Monique was actually right."

"What?"

She continued to huff and puff. "Nothing."

The nurses hurriedly wrapped the babe and laid her in her mother's arms.

Happy tears wet Kayla's cheeks. "She's so pretty."

Jude took in the full head of dark hair. "Looks just like her mama." He caressed his newborn baby girl. "Hey, precious. It's nice to finally meet you."

The child quieted and did her best to focus on his face.

"Look at that," said one of the nurses. "She knows her daddy's voice."

Jude's heart filled with more pride than he'd thought possible—even more than it had at his and Kayla's wedding last month.

He again kissed Kayla's chapped lips. Poor thing. For the last twelve hours, she'd had nothing but ice chips. "You did great, sweetheart."

Peering up at him with more love than he deserved, she said, "Not without your help."

Once the baby was weighed, measured, swaddled and placed into her mother's waiting arms, Jude excused himself and made his way down the hall to the waiting room. All eyes were on him as he entered. Dad and Hillary, his brothers and their wives, Kayla's mother, Claudette—who'd flown in for the wedding and returned last week for the birth—and Joe and Maureen Bradshaw.

Jude tried to contain his excitement, but this was one event that simply couldn't be contained. "It's a girl," he unashamedly blurted out. "Ten fingers, ten toes, six pounds, thirteen ounces, nineteen inches long."

A variety of cheers erupted around the room, along with a round of applause.

"You'll all get to meet her soon enough, but the grandparents get to go first."

He led all five of them—Dad and Hillary, Joe and Maureen and Claudette—to Kayla's room. Once inside, he accepted his daughter from Kayla while the family hugged and congratulated her. Then, as they clustered together, he proudly showed them his little girl.

"I'd like you all to meet Avery Mona Stephens."

While the women cooed and fussed over her, Jude didn't miss the tears that filled his father's eyes.

Having observed them, too, Kayla reached for the old man's hand. "Mona was very special to both of us."

Still holding Avery, Jude approached the Bradshaws first. "Would you like to hold your granddaughter?"

Maureen's eyes sparkled with unshed tears. "Oh, yes. Yes, I would."

Jude placed the babe in her arms as the woman spoke sweetly to her first grandchild.

Beside her, Joe's grizzly bear persona transformed into a teddy bear as he tenderly reached his large finger to the baby's tiny fist. Since November, he'd been attending anger management classes, determined to break the cycle that had sought to destroy his family. "I do believe you are the sweetest thing I've ever seen, little Avery."

Jude moved beside his wife and gave her another kiss. "You're amazing, you know that."

"I don't know, I'd say you're pretty amazing, too. I mean, you're working almost single-handedly to have our new house move-in ready by summer."

"At least until you put me to work on the hotel."

"Yeah, about that." A mischievous grin split her pretty face. "You start Monday."

"Oh, really." His last day with the police force had been two days before they got married. Since then he'd been juggling his woodworking, the new house and the hotel while they continued to live in his grandmother's house.

"Surely you don't expect me to be on the job?"

"I suppose you can be a lady of leisure for a few weeks."

Her chestnut eyes sparkled up at him. "I love you."

"I love you, too." He smiled at Kayla, knowing that this was the life they'd both dreamed of. And though they'd taken a roundabout way to get there, God had brought them back together. This time, it was forever.

* * * * *

*Look for the next book in
the Rocky Mountain Heroes series
by Mindy Obenhaus,
available March 2020 wherever
Harlequin Love Inspired books
and ebooks are sold.*

Dear Reader,

As I contemplated Jude, the fourth brother in my Rocky Mountain Heroes series, I knew he'd had his heart broken by a lost love and that he still carried a torch for that woman. But imagine coming face-to-face with that person again, only to discover that she's pregnant! And thus began Jude's journey.

The power of love as God intended it—patient, kind, protective, trusting, hopeful and persevering—is hard to resist. Having been wounded both emotionally and physically in the name of love, Kayla had to rediscover love the way God meant it to be. And Jude was more than happy to show her.

I hope you enjoyed this story as much as I did. I like watching people fall in love, but there was something special about this couple. Perhaps it was the desire to see Kayla find her way home to the kind of love she so deserved.

The next and final story in this series belongs to Daniel. And I have a feeling the youngest Stephens brother's tale is going to pack the biggest punch yet.

Until then, I would love to hear from you. You can contact me via my website, mindyobenhaus.com, or you can snail-mail me c/o Love Inspired Books, 195 Broadway, 24th Floor, New York, NY 10007.

See you next time,
Mindy